Stories from the Barrio and Other 'Hoods

◆

For Mimi —

I hope these
stories make you
smile.

Your El Paso friend

Margarita Perez

01/10/02

Stories from the Barrio and Other 'Hoods

◆

Margarita B. Velez

Writers Club Press
San Jose New York Lincoln Shanghai

Stories from the Barrio and Other 'Hoods

Writers Club Press
an imprint of iUniverse.com, Inc.

For information address:
iUniverse.com, Inc.
5220 S 16th, Ste. 200
Lincoln, NE 68512
www.iuniverse.com

ISBN: 0-595-18745-5

Printed in the United States of America

Dedication

◆

This book is dedicated with love to the memory of my mother, Maria Noriega Barrera, my husband, Bob, my daughter Laura, sons Rob, Mike and Vince and Bianca, my niece. I hope that my grandchildren will read and learn about our family through these reminisces. The stories belong to all the Mamas, Papas, brothers and sisters, *Abuelitas, Abuelitos, Tios, Tias, comadres, compadres,* cousins and transients who wandered through the neighborhood, struggled to move out and carry the barrio in their hearts.

Acknowledgements

◆

Without the people etched in my memory this book would not be possible. I thank every member of my family, young and old, the neighbors and those who left a mark on my life without even knowing it. My memories weave deliciously through different neighborhoods like the aroma of tortillas cooking on the griddle. If you find yourself in my recollections, thank you for sharing part of your life. I am grateful to Leon Metz, the El Paso Herald Post, Southwest Woman, and especially The El Paso Times for publishing my work. Finally I thank all the people who said they related to my memories although they grew up in other parts of the country. It is for you that the recesses of my mind were explored to evoke the memories that belong to all of us.

Contents

◆

Beginnings

◆

My grandparents fled Mexico in 1915 as the revolution tore their native land apart. Heading north they toted an infant who would grow up to be my father. Upon arriving in the United States they settled in El Paso's Second Ward among immigrants like themselves whose dreams and hopes for a better life they shared.

As a child I heard *Abuelita* reminisce about *"mi tierra,"* the land she left never to return. I listened as she talked about raising a large family. Tales involving my father's antics always made me laugh. I remember the pained look that masked her face as she talked about sending four sons to fight in foreign lands with names like Karachi, India, Malinta Hill and Germany. But a cheerful countenance replaced it when she talked about their triumphant return after World War II. She spoke about the medals pinned on their chests by a grateful nation for her sons' gallantry and valor. Growing up in her midst enriched my life.

My childhood in the barrio was memorable and colorful. Love abounded and everybody cared about everybody else. The neighbors looked after the children, keeping an eye on us as we walked to and from school and rejoicing with our achievements. The watchful eye of so many guardians also encouraged us to walk a straight line.

As they prospered my uncles moved their families to other parts of the city where we discovered other cultures. When I started first grade Spanish was my primary language but Papa insisted that we learn English and it became my second tongue. If the sting of discrimination arose, it only made me strive harder to succeed. By the time I completed the twelfth grade, the four grade schools and three high schools on my record had given me a broad view of life in El Paso. Entrance into the business world helped to widen my perspective and enhance my views.

After marriage I left El Paso and gained a new appreciation for my hometown and returned here by choice. I love this diverse city and write about the people and places that have touched my life in many special ways. My memories will strike a chord with other El Pasoans. I think the story of my name; Margarita is interesting. In Mexican calendars, June 10, my birthday is attributed to Santa Margarita. Mama was keen on giving us the saint's name of the day on which we were born. My sisters and I were lucky that our birthdays fell on saint's days we like; Margarita, Maria de los Angeles and Maria Elena, but my brothers were never quite happy with their monikers. Eusebio was born December 16 and Papa didn't like the name but Mama insisted. Exactly a year later, a second brother was born and now it was Papa's insistence that gave his son the saint's name too. So my two brothers are named Eusebio. Luckily my parents also gave them a middle name.

When I was little girl Papa tagged me "Margie" and the name stuck. Now that I'm older I don't particularly like "Margie" and have tried to shed it but thought that people would not recognize me by Margarita. Several years ago I was encouraged when Ruthie Kay, a prominent El Pasoan announced that henceforth she would answer only to Katherine. She made it stick and so should I.

Margarita represents what El Paso is all about; a blend of cultures, like a savory and spicy salsa. My aim is to summon memories of the city we all love and I hope that my musings will prove entertaining and thought provoking.

November 1996

Is It Fideo or Vermicelli?

◆

When I was growing up in El Paso, our town was extending to the northeast desert. Fort Bliss was a vital link in America's defense and fast becoming an integral part of the community. Men were home from the war, basking in the warmth of a country at peace, raising families and contributing to the city's growth.

My grandparents were immigrants who fled Mexico during the revolution and later bought a home close to Fort Bliss just within the city limits. On meager earnings, they reared seven sons and three daughters. Four of the boys served honorably in World War II while the young ones served in Korea and in the Vietnam conflict.

As the family multiplied by marriage and grandchildren, the tradition to visit grandparents weekly was honored by all. The grandkids frolicked in the sprawling yard and vast desert behind their house.

Our entertainment was simple; we climbed the mountains and explored the desert's beauty. Once we laboriously dug out a barrel cactus for *Abuelita* who used it to make a delicious Mexican candy. The Del Norte Drive-In Theatre charged a ten-cent walk-in price and, as regular customers, we brought pillows and blankets to endure the hard cement benches provided for pedestrian moviegoers.

We tried to befriend Lizzie, an eccentric woman of unknown age, recognizable in long skirts, a sun- bonnet and the red wagon she pulled wherever she went. Paul's Café on Dyer Street catered mainly to the soldiers from Fort Bliss but also delighted our palates with nickel ice cream cones. As teenagers, we haunted Swanky Franky's for pizza and enjoyed the latest rock-and-roll hits on the jukebox.

As one of the first Mexican-American families to descend on this Anglo section of El Paso, we were sometimes treated like foreigners and heard derogatory slurs about our ethnicity and the broken phrases we spoke. In spite of that, eventually we found long lasting friendship and respect.

The kids who taunted us as "dirty Mexicans" later became our best friends. Jimmy, Johnny, and Tubby were freckled-faced brothers who derided our broken English and called us names. As I waited for popcorn one night at the drive in's snack bar, they called me a "dirty Mexican," whereupon I nastily retorted, "you dirty white trash!" A fracas ensued where my cousins and I shoved, punched and kicked the three blond rascals.

Despite Mama's admonitions that girls must never fight, I punched Tubby in the mouth and his lip bled. That stopped the melee and after tending to his wound, a new friendship blossomed between us. Like other American kids we were soon running in and out of each other's homes, often sitting at the family table to share a meal. Tubby learned to eat Mexican food and flour tortillas right off Grandma's griddle and my first taste of hominy grits was at his house. Tubby also learned a little Spanish and one day said, "*Te amo, Abuelita*," and there was no question that he had come to love my grandmother. When Tubby tragically drowned before his fifteenth birthday, I grieved as though I'd lost my brother. But as Grandma and I prayed the rosary in the Baptist Church, no one treated us like strangers anymore; we had become as close as family.

Only two stores served the area – Nabhan's Grocery Store and Shapley's Groceries. One day when Grandma sent me to buy "fideo," a family pasta favorite, it seemed only logical that the store would have it. To my consternation when I asked Mr. Shapley for the item, he didn't recognize it. After long moments of dialog, he finally gave up and said, "Go look, maybe you'll find it, I don't know what it is."

I searched up and down the aisles until at last, there among packages of macaroni and spaghetti, I found it! I pointed to the printed red words; "Fideo Vermicelli" printed prominently against the yellow package as Mr. Shapley smiled at my find.

"Vermicelli," he exclaimed rubbing his chin, "You call it fideo but I call it vermicelli!" On subsequent visits we often bantered about vermicelli and fideo and today I still remember the shopkeeper fondly.

The weekly tradition to visit our grandparents continued despite the long and tedious bus ride to their house. One Sunday on the return trip we boarded a bus crowded with GIs on liberty pass headed for downtown El Paso.

Finding a vacant seat, I surrendered it to *Tia Chencha* and a man in the adjacent seat gallantly gave his up. *Tia Chencha* wanted the seat for *Tia Chita* who was traveling with us and began to beckon her. The passengers were mostly Anglo men and *Tia Chencha* later explained that she didn't want to sound conspicuous when she called *Chita* who swayed from a strap at the front of the bus. She added an anglicized twist to the name as she confidently called, "Shit...Shit..come here...there's a vacant seat."

Muffled snickering erupted from the other passengers. *Tia Chencha* was confused but persisted with her urgent call. "Shit...Shit..." rang out comically while a red-faced *Tia Chita* tried vainly to ignore it as the crescendo of laughter mounted. Finally *Tia Chita* stormed down the aisle, angrily dropped on the seat and loudly chastised her sister's ignorance. Meekly we all witnessed the mortification that flooded them both when *Tia Chita* explained to a chagrined *Tia Chencha* exactly what she had been calling her.

That incident propelled us to master the English language. Now if we stumble on a word we chuckle and forge ahead. We're proud, loyal, bilingual citizens of the America our fathers went to war for. We haven't forgotten where we came from or how we struggled to succeed.

Tia Chencha speaks English flawlessly and today recounts the incident with relish. We profited fromZ her ability to laugh at herself and from the perseverance that inspired her to learn the language. The episode proved that it's essential to speak this nation's tongue, not necessarily to assimilate but to become better citizens and more productive Americans. *Tia Chita* laughs sheepishly when the story is recounted but is glad that it motivated us to improve our lot.

As we accepted the diversity of other cultures we enriched our own. When we laughed as we tripped on words like "chair" and "share" our sense of humor helped us to appreciate the value of communication. By sharing our friend's hominy grits and collard greens we accepted them totally, and in giving of ourselves, we flung open the door of friendship and understanding.

Our country provides many learning opportunities and only when we allow it do the difference of our backgrounds get in the way. It's not necessary to forsake the culture or language of our heritage to become part of the melting pot; but it behooves us all to master English if we are to become articulate role models for our children. As we master America's tongue we must encourage others to persevere and also be willing to shoulder the burden of the war against illiteracy. Active participation in this battle will serve as an example for those who struggle and are at risk today.

Although Grandmother never mastered her adopted country's tongue, she encouraged us to pursue education and set an example with her constant quest to learn. She praised and exalted each of our accomplishments no matter how small and she earned love and respect through her neighborliness. Her English vocabulary was limited but it included "I can, I will and I must."

Therefore I will and I must be a soldier in this war against illiteracy by helping others become proficient bilingual citizens. After all, neighborliness is also an integral part of my heritage. Grandma was the perfect example of a neighbor and I wouldn't want to disappoint her. May she rest in peace.

August 1995

Celia from Sedalia

◆

It was Thanksgiving and Mama was struggling to make ends meet as a single parent the year I finished high school. I helped mash the potatoes while Mama made biscuits and heated the dark and light turkey slices she brought home from her job at the school cafeteria. She stirred the gravy and put the cranberry sauce in my favorite relish tray.

The table was covered with a tablecloth Mama had ironed with cooked starched the night before. My sister Angie brought in colorful chrysanthemums from Mama's garden while younger sister Mary brought paper cut-outs depicting a pilgrim boy and girl she colored in her first grade class. We arranged them in the middle of the table and admired our centerpiece.

After saying grace Mama served generous portions of our bountiful meal. I had just buttered my biscuit when Mary wondered out loud, "How come we don't carve a roasted turkey like they did on 'Father Knows Best?'" My knife hovered in midair as I looked from one sibling to the other. Mama calmly replied, "Because it's a lot easier to have the turkey already sliced." Mary was satisfied while I marveled at Mama's wisdom.

We had homemade pumpkin pie with whipped cream for dessert and forgot my sister's question. Later we watched a football game and ate cold turkey sandwiches and more pie.

The next day I went back to work at my new job Downtown and during coffee break I asked Celia, a tall, shy co-worker about her turkey dinner. She was from Sedalia, Missouri and lived with her sister and Army captain husband at Fort Bliss. I envisioned a roasted turkey served in an elegant dining room on the military post.

Sadness filled her eyes when Celia said "I took my niece to the Oasis and we had chili beans and cornbread. My sister and her husband had an argument."

"Chili beans at the Oasis on Thanksgiving Day?" The image of lonely souls pained me and I quickly extended an invitation. "We have lots of leftover turkey and trimmings, I bet Mama would make biscuits if you came over for dinner."

Celia accepted and after work we rode the bus to my home in Northeast El Paso laughing and talking all the way. When we arrived, Mama had biscuits and a bowl of mashed potatoes ready. Gravy was simmering on the range and the aroma of turkey filled the air.

The family welcomed my friend. "Look at my pilgrims," Mary urged while the dog nudged our guest. When we offered thanks for a second turkey dinner, I was especially grateful to have plenty to share. By dessert time, Celia already had lost her shyness.

After dinner my brother pulled out the Scrabble board and we cleared the table while Mama crocheted in the next room. We laughed when Celia searched for multiple letter words as we deciphered five-character ones. The game ended when my brother used all his tiles to spell our EQUIVOCATION for a double word and bonus point. Celia was impressed but we told her that he liked to read the dictionary and reveled in showing off.

When it was time to leave Celia gave Mama a friendly hug and my brother a warm two-handed handshake. Her eyes misted when she thanked me and said it was the best Thanksgiving she'd ever had.

Celia quit work and left suddenly before Christmas. Although she promised to stay in touch, I never heard from her again.

Every year I count among my blessings that shy young lady from Sedalia, MO who helped me see how truly blessed my life has been.

November 1996

Death

◆

I was eight years old when my baby sister died just a few days after we had blown out the candle celebrating her first birthday.

She was a fair-haired child with sparkling eyes who gurgled when I pushed her in the baby carriage. Then she became ill and despite Mama's loving care, her condition worsened and she was hospitalized. Every day Mama would go to the hospital, leaving us at home where *Abuelita* provided grandmotherly care.

On a hot June day Mama returned with the news that her baby girl had died. I couldn't believe that my healthy sister who squealed with delight when she rode in the baby carriage was dead. Dead! I hardly understood the meaning of the word, but knew that I'd never cuddle the sweet child again.

Suddenly the sun disappeared and the wind howled, scattering litter and dust in a dark mass that matched the black cloud that engulfed our home. Hot, dusty days still make me blue.

Funeral arrangements were made and the family walked from the barrio to the funeral home at Campbell and Myrtle Streets. Adults led the pilgrimage with children dressed in Sunday best trailing behind. The girls wore white dresses and I remember feeling festive among my friends and relatives.

Along the way people stood at their doors to watch the procession. Our white dresses were bright against the mourning black when someone asked, "*Van a ofrecer flores?*" The onlooker thought we were going to church to offer flowers to the Virgin Mary.

"No, it's my baby sister's funeral," I replied with a big smile. A woman standing at the door shook her head and disappeared inside.

Shortly thereafter, a playmate's father died and the wake was held in the family's living room. Chairs were pushed against the wall with the casket occupying the middle of the room. People approached the sad widow to whisper condolences.

Outside I joined my Uncle Pete who was only a year older to crowd with other kids against the screen door for a better view. I could see my little friend inside playing with a toy truck and heard him making engine noises while his mother tried to stop him.

"*Dios te salve Maria…*" Mama and Grandmother recited the rosary with other mourners. The crucifixes dangled in the candlelight as the beads moved through their fingers.

We pressed against the screen for a better view until someone urged us to move away. At first we didn't budge but the man's stern voice finally compelled us to step back.

My uncle stood up, stiffened beside me and said, "*No le hace, cuando se muera mi papa, no voy a dejar entrar a nadie…*" My grandmother gasped with horror on hearing her youngest child declare that when his father died, he wasn't going to let anybody in. The mourners tittered and Mama covered her mouth.

Without a word *Abuelita* walked out and marched us home. Uncle Pete's outrageous retort had ruined the solemn ritual.

As troubling as death can be it is more confusing when children don't understand and get no explanation. My parents refused an autopsy for their baby and we never knew what killed her. At my tender age, I thought the funeral was a festive parade instead of a gloomy, final trek.

Uncle Pete's feelings were hurt when the funeral wake excluded us from a perceived social event and he reacted in anger. Now my blissful ignorance and Uncle Pete's mischief make me smile, albeit a bit chagrined.

February 1997

Stealing *Abuelito's* Bicycle

◆

Grandfather was a tall, lean man who rode a big black bicycle when he came to visit. He looked handsome riding up in a dark coat with black hair shining against his light complexion. I remember his smile although he didn't often show it. He was widowed early and left with four young children to care for. My mother at six was the youngest and I imagine his load was heavy and kept him from smiling.

He played a significant role in my life and I cherish the times we spent together. He lived alone in an apartment not far from our house and I'd drop by to visit after school. Afflicted by asthma, he was often confined to bed but always welcomed me.

When he came to our home Mama doted on him and demonstrated her love in those special ways that daughters do. She'd brew a fresh pot of coffee and bustled about preparing his favorite meal. Their easy talking was reassuring as he sipped hot coffee in the small kitchen while Mama worked on the meal. Before long the aroma of flour tortillas and simmering spices wafted throughout the house.

When Grandfather arrived he left his bicycle outside the door, unlocked. The bicycle looked so big that many times I wondered if I'd be able to ride it. One day the temptation was too much and I "borrowed" the bike.

Quietly I walked the bicycle away from the door and then peddled happily down the street. Back and forth I rode, raising dust as I peddled faster. My pigtails flew as I made wide turns at the end of the street. Over and over I rode, waving to friends walking by.

As I headed back to return the bicycle, I noticed Mama standing outside the door. Her mouth was tight and her hands were on her hips as she eyed me on her father's bike.

I pedaled very slowly hoping she'd step back inside but she seemed rooted to the spot. Mama's stance told me it was time for me to face the music.

"I just took a ride…" I stammered and leaned the bicycle against the wall. Without a word she took my arm and led me inside where she started scolding me.

"You stole my father's bicycle," she said. My stomach knotted up and my mind protested against the word "stole." I kept quiet as she admonished against taking things without permission.

I looked at my grandfather who sipped coffee but listened to every word. My body quivered with shame and I ran to him.

"*Abuelito,* I'm sorry, I just wanted to see if I could ride a big bike." I blurted penitently.

His brown eyes were filled with sadness as he looked at Mama and then back to me. Tears streamed down my face and the pigtails dangled as I hung my head.

When I looked up into my grandfather's eyes again, relief swept over me. His face broke into that rare smile and his arms wrapped around me.

"There, there, no more tears, it's just a bicycle," he murmured.

Mama's admonishment continued but with me sheltered in his arms her words didn't sting as much. Grandfather told me to ask before borrowing his bike again. And, on subsequent visits, I did.

When my birthday arrived, my parents surprised me with a bright red girl's bicycle. I suspect it was Mama's way of ensuring that the "borrowing" would end.

January 1997

Dinero Isn't *Dinner*

◆

Mispronounced words and different accents punctuate our conversation and make life interesting. Whenever I hear a slip of the tongue, it reminds me of my own experiences and I smile. It's also a good way to start a conversation.

Mother's only sister speaks English with a pronounced accent. *Tia Luz* is a petite shy woman who boosts my ego and brings joy to my life.

A favorite memory is the day when she was visiting as I sauntered in wearing a bright yellow dress. Looking up, *Tia Luz* exclaimed, "*Ay mija, que bonita te ves en jello.*" The vision of me squiggling in lemon gelatin made me smile. But, I knew that her compliment meant that I looked good in the "yellow" dress. Another time she said, "Margie *es muy esmart.*" Her words are etched in my mind and give me encouragement.

My friend Mike lived in Central America when his father served with the Foreign Service. At a formal dinner, Mike was trying out his high-school Spanish with a diplomat's daughter while her mother eyed them closely. Mike said something that caused the young lady to blush and he fumbled for the Spanish word for "embarrass."

"*Perdone que la embarase, Senorita.*" Mike said with confidence. The mother gasped in horror and the young lady stiffened as fat tears spilled from her blazing eyes. In trying to apologize for embarrassing the girl, Mike instead had apologized for make her pregnant. It took a lot of diplomacy on his father's part to explain Mike's faux pas.

Tia Ester was riding the bus when a seatmate asked for the time. *Tia* was about to tell her it was 8:30 but didn't know the English word for half past the hour. Silently she remembered that *"media"* means "stocking" and "half" in Spanish. My aunt declared, "It's eight and stocking." Her companion looked perplexed. *Tia Ester* picked the wrong word. My aunt let her read the time for herself and remembers her companion's warm smile of understanding.

As a young boy, my father was working for a non-Spanish speaker. Papa was learning to speak English but didn't yet know the word for money. When he went to ask for his pay, Papa struggled for the term, but couldn't come up with it. *"Dinero*...dinner..." He decided to anglicize the word and said, "I want my dinner."

The kindly woman brought him a sandwich. Papa ate it and then asked for his "dinner" again. The woman brought him another sandwich. Papa polished off the second serving with much less enthusiasm then asked for his "dinner" again. The confused woman questioned him about his insatiable hunger. Papa was frustrated but undaunted. He decided not to say "dinner" again.

In Spanish he requested *"mi dinero"* and rubbed his thumb over his fingers in the familiar gesture meaning money. Finally the woman's face lit up and she rushed for her purse. Papa chuckled when he told how the woman hurriedly paid him and sent him on his way.

At a PTA installation ceremony in front of a large crowd, I once said, "leadersheep" instead of leadership. When snickers rose from the audience my face turned red. Looking at the crowd I hesitated then remembered my father's experience and cleared my throat, smiled, pronounced the word properly and went on with my speech.

Laughing at our mistakes helps us overcome embarrassment and we can learn from the experience. Sometimes if I stumble with "ch" and "sh" and mispronounce "share" or "Charlotte" you might hear me say "the taco slipped out" just before my smile turns into laughter.

November 1997

The Thread that Binds

◆

Children's voices shouted, "*La pastilla, la pastilla, donde esta la pastilla?*" as we exited Saint Ignatius Church after the baptismal of a young relative. Papa, the godfather, tossed nickels and dimes in the air while kids scampered to snatch up the money.

Later I learned that if the godfather didn't toss the coins or "*pastilla,*" the kids proclaimed that the child being baptized would suffer from colic. That's one of my first memories of a religious ceremony.

Dona Gabriela, our neighbor, was called "*Jaleluya,*" a crude description of a non-Catholic. She hosted worshippers at her home where the tinkering piano drew the neighborhood children to listen outside. We lingered beyond the screen door and sang along. They always concluded with "The Battle Hymn of the Republic." Later it dawned on me where the moniker for "*Los Jaleluyas*" derived from.

For my first Holy Communion I wore a floor-length gown and used it the next year to offer flowers to the Holy Mother. As we passed their homes women handed us flowers from their gardens. We arrived at church laden with fragrant roses, carnations and sunny marigolds which always made me sneeze.

Later we attended St. Francis Xavier Church and as an adolescent, "*Las Hijas de Maria*" provided direction. Father Diego guided the voices of the "Daughters of Mary" to sing High Mass in Latin. Now I make a special trip to Christ the King Monastery to rekindle that old feeling.

When Jehovah's Witnesses came knocking, Papa invited them in. They quoted from the bible and left copies of the Watchtower, which we read avidly. Their weekly visits helped us to define the difference between our beliefs.

One hot day as we frolicked in the sprinkler in our grandparent's lawn, a minister stopped to announce summer Bible School at the Church of the Nazarene. *Abuelita*, our grandmother, said we would attend.

Every morning for the next week, my cousins and I waited for the bus to take us to the church on Dyer Street. Later we sang "Jesus loves me, this I know for the Bible tells me so" for *Abuelita* even though she didn't understand English. My aunt was aghast when she heard we had gone to Bible School. "How could you allow them to go to the Protestant church," she protested. *Abuelita* replied, "As long as they learn about God there is no harm." No more was said, Abuelita was right.

The father of a high school friend was a Lutheran Chaplain at Fort Bliss. They invited me to service and explained the service to help broaden my understanding. Sikh members were also hospitable when I attended services with my friend Jagdev.

My neighbor Laniece provides tickets for the Living Singing Christmas tree at the First Baptist Church. Multicolored lights twinkle while voices blend in joyous song bringing the tree to life. It's a wonderful Yuletide gift.

In May, members of all denominations gather for the Northeast Prayer Breakfast. For more than twenty years, this event has united the community to break bread, share the gospel and honor the Citizen and Family of the year.

I'm lucky that friends care enough to share their faith. By attending various services I learned tolerance and respect for different beliefs.

Abuelita was right, as long as you worship God the blending of faith brings amazing grace.

May 1997

Easter Ego Booster

◆

As a teenager I spent one spring with my aunt, uncle and their sons. I thought they were rich because they owned a small business, had fancy furniture, and a maid who tended to all their needs. At home Mama did all the work although I helped. Now Mina, the maid, had breakfast ready when I got up.

The damask cloth on the dining table was bright and the crystal in the cherrywood cabinet glittered in the morning sun. At my place a grapefruit half topped with a maraschino cherry awaited me. But it was the little silver grapefruit spoon that got my attention. We didn't have anything like that although Mama often served grapefruit. I was impressed.

After breakfast, we gathered our books and instead of walking, *Tio Lorenzo* drove us to school. When my cousins bickered in the back seat I acted as mediator and it made me feel "grown up."

After school we'd sit at the dining table to do our homework. When my cousins needed it, I helped with their assignment and together we worked on arithmetic problems. A special bond blossomed between us that spring.

During Holy Week, school let out and we spent idle time watching television. Thursday, *Tia Angela* handed me fifty dollars and suggested I go shopping for an Easter outfit. Fifty Bucks! I couldn't believe that all that money was just for me.

The wind blew dust everywhere and I tied a scarf around my head to keep my hair from flying in my face. As I walked from the Popular to the

White House admiring spring fashions the money in my pocket made me feel like the rich Veronica from Archie Comics fame. At Gilbert's I hesitated because normally I couldn't afford their clothes. But now, with fifty dollars in my purse, I pranced right it.

A young woman helped me find my size and I spotted a linen suit the color of ripe peaches. The clerk brought a contrasting blouse and when I tried it on, we agreed it was perfect.

I walked out carrying a large white bag emblazoned with brown GILBERT'S lettering. I still had money to buy shoes to complete my ensemble.

When I returned home, *Tia Angela* was reading the newspaper and smiled her approval when I showed off my purchases. She wouldn't take the change remaining from the fifty dollars so I tucked in my patched suede purse.

On Easter Sunday Mina saw me in the suit and declared that peach was a good color for me.

My cousin whistled and said, "You look pretty." And that's how I truly felt.

Adolescence is a confusing time but with a touch of understanding, *Tia Angela* gave me a real ego boost. I wore that outfit until it was threadbare but the good feeling remains today.

Many years passed and the opportunity to do the same for someone else came along. My pre-teen niece pointed out a special dress she wanted. I brought it home for her and as her eyes sparkled I knew that her ego had been enhanced. How lucky I am to be able to share good times and fortune. Thanks, *Tia Angela* for setting the example by giving that special gift so many years ago.

March 1997

Abuelita's Spirit

◆

It was Mother's Day and long-distance calls from our absent children delayed us for Sunday Mass. Their greetings were heartwarming and welcomed but deepened my lonely feelings. Mother was recovering from pneumonia and I felt sad that she was unable to worship with us.

We arrived at Blessed Sacrament Catholic Church as the entrance song joyously filled the air. I spotted women accompanied by their children and felt a tug at my heart.

Silently I knelt to offer the Mass for my mother's recovery and for all mothers. Reaching for the book to find the day's readings, I noticed a lady had quietly joined us in the pew. Elderly and petite, she had a white orchid pinned to her pretty blue-and-white polka-dotted dress. Her head was bowed in prayer and I saw that her hair was plaited into a bun.

An image of my grandmother, Jesusita Mares Barrera, wearing her long tresses in a similar fashion flashed into my mind. At the Gloria, we rose, and the rosary beads the lady carried caught my eye. Her small wrinkled hands reminded me of my grandmother and as Mass progressed, I recalled the many lessons learned at her side.

I remembered her blessing before I walked up the aisle to marry the man of my dreams. A few weeks after my joyous wedding day, she had been cruelly snatched away by a deadly tumor that swallowed her brain and extinguished the light that gave inspiration to her children, grandchildren and anyone lucky enough to have been in her presence. Years later, the void she left remains in my heart.

At the Lord's Prayer, I reached for the little lady's frail hand while more memories flooded my mind. I wanted to hug the little stranger. Suddenly, she pulled my hand to her lips, kissed it and smiled.

Our eyes locked in unspoken understanding as tears trailed unabashedly down my face. Glancing at my husband I saw moisture gather in his eyes and when he squeezed my hand, I knew that he had felt my joy. At the sign of peace I embraced the little lady whispering "Thank you." She beamed and patted my hand.

My faith teaches that in communion we receive the body and blood of Christ in the unleavened wafer and sip of wine. I felt a presence walking beside me as I approached the altar to receive communion. With tranquility I received those gifts and was thankful for all the blessings of my life. Returning to my seat I knelt and prayed for Grandmother, whose comforting spirit reached out to me in my moment of utter loneliness.

Grandmother transmitted her love through the little stranger sharing the pew on Mother's Day. When Mass ended the little lady had disappeared. Although I always look for her I've never seen her again.

May 1996

Hamburger Joints and Doughnuts

◆

The gimmicks of fast food restaurants sometimes make me yearn for the hamburger joints of my youth. Lucky Boy in Downtown El Paso served oversized hamburgers with a special sauce that made your mouth water and the Charcoaler remains a favorite from those days of old.

Yet the one that lingers deliciously in my mind is an establishment managed by an uncle on Alameda Street. After school, my brother and I would sometimes visit *Tio Lorenzo*, a quiet man with twinkling eyes and an engaging smile.

We'd find him behind the counter grilling burgers where all could see. He welcomed us with a smile that always reminded me of Mama. He'd grill a couple of hamburgers and then come around the counter to sit with us. His favorite meal was a hamburger steak topped with chili beans and a side order of hash brown potatoes.

"How was school," he always asked, and quizzed us on math and smiled at our responses to his science questions. In the background, *Tia Angela* could be heard admonishing a waitress for some infraction.

Tio Lorenzo would take a slice of lemon meringue pie from the refrigerated glass case and pour a cup of coffee. He offered us pie which we declined but only because we planned to have dessert elsewhere.

Sometimes *Tia Angela* joined us and always asked about the family. Our visits were special times when relatives encouraged our education by spurring our curiosity.

We left the restaurant and walked down the street to the Sun Bakery, where our grandfather was a master baker. Don Marcos, our paternal *Abuelo*, baked doughnuts, *pan dulce* and *campechanas,* a flight flaky pastry that melted in my mouth. His toothless smile revealed he was glad to see us.

"How do you make the doughnuts?" My brother once asked and sent *Abuelito* into a long discussion. He explained how flour was mixed with yeast and eggs and left to rise. We watched him punch a great mound of dough with flair. Then his strong arms kneaded and left it to rise again. The mixture swelled and we watched as our grandfather rolled it out and cut the doughnuts with a special tool. He placed them beside the hot oven and doughy circles puffed up again. Then Grandfather fried them in hot oil until they were golden brown.

There among the bakers we sat on turned over milk crates and feasted on warm sugary doughnuts and cold milk.

Those visits were special bonding times. He always made time for us although Mama tried to keep us from visiting him too much. *Abuelito* sent us home with a bag full of assorted pastries selected from the cooling racks. My brother and I ate dessert all the way home because it was impossible to resist the temptation.

We met friends along the way and shared doughnuts and *empanadas,* the fruit fritters that were my brother's favorite. By the time we arrived home the bag was half full because we'd been so generous.

We were scolded for arriving late from school and Mama asked us to curtail the visits to our working kin. But those were special times and our school chums urged us to take the intentional detour to the bakery because we shared the flavorful pastries.

I still go to the Hamburger Hut for the best hamburger in town and savor the memory of carefree days when the food lured you in instead of slick commercials with cartoon characters and catchy tunes.

June 1997

Sunday Drives into Adventure

◆

At my husband's suggestion we took a Sunday drive in the country. Mama and my niece Bianca rode in the back seat as we meandered along Socorro Road toward the outskirts of El Paso County. We stopped at the San Elizario Mission and lamented the falling plaster and the painted toenails on the angels holding the holy water at the entrance of the historic church.

Along the road we passed cotton and alfalfa fields and Bianca recognized the corn swaying in the breeze. Mama laughed when I remembered that when we were kids Papa us took on excursions to discover the agriculture of El Paso's Lower Valley. Our family didn't have a car but we'd board the blue and white bus at San Jacinto Plaza and ride to the end of the line. Then Papa would lead us along dirt paths until he found a picnic spot.

Papa told us about the different crops and helped us understand the gifts of the good earth. We were city folks let loose in the farm, squealing at the sight and smell of animals recognized from schoolbooks. I still remember the taste of sweet corn right off the stalk.

On one particular excursion we rode as far as Clint, Texas. After the long trip we found a shady spot and ate tacos Mama had prepared and drank ice cold Coca-Colas that Papa bought at a gas station. We tossed stones into an irrigation ditch while Mama and Papa sat beneath the shade of a cottonwood tree. That idyllic moment is still fresh in my mind.

The sun was beginning its descent when we returned to the bus stop and discovered that the last bus had already left. I was always a worrier and asked, "How are we going to get home?"

But Papa had a ready answer. "I'll find a way, don't you worry." Tears were already gathering in my eyes when Papa went off to find a way home. Mama comforted me but didn't seem perturbed. Soon Papa returned in a car whose driver took us closer into town where we caught the bus back to El Paso.

Sunday drives are almost as rare as those memorable bus rides when we learned about country life and Papa's resourcefulness.

One day I told a friend about our trips to the country and suddenly he roared with laughter. His family lived on a farm in the Lower Valley and he laughed because his mother would bring him in the blue bus to experience city life in El Paso.

The irony made us smile as we compared memories about the food that our mothers packed for the long rides.

On our recent Sunday drive, we crossed the narrow international bridge into Caseta, Mexico. The restaurant on the main street was closed and people were leaving church after Mass. Fresh fruit drinks were sold next to a hat stand while an assortment of musical cassette tapes seemed to blister in the hot afternoon sun. After a brief tour we approached the port of entry where a huge sign warned against smuggling parrots, oranges and pork meat.

That long ride made us hungry and we left the green fields of Fabens and headed to Cattleman's to dine on the famous juicy steaks and huge baked potatoes.

Papa's adventurous spirit lingered in my mind and I yearned to follow his tracks. Looking out into the barren desert surrounding the dude ranch I wondered what exciting stories he would've contrived to stimulate our minds and whet our scientific curiosity.

July 1997

Papa's Lunchpail

◆

When we were kids Mama rose early to prepare the lunch that she lovingly packed in Papa's lunch pail. Sleepily I heard the "clack, clack" of the wooden rolling pin against the board as she rolled out flour tortillas. Delicious aromas tickled my senses before I woke up.

Mama hummed as she rolled out the tortillas and Papa strummed the guitar between sips of coffee. The radio was always tuned to XELO's *"El Gallito Madrugador,"* where a rooster's feisty "cock-a-doodle-doo" rang out as punctually as an alarm clock. That memory lingers in my mind.

Papa toted a black steel lunch pail that had room for a Thermos bottle held in place by a curved steel retainer. The fresh, hot tortillas were wrapped around *"Huevos con chorizo,"* a tasty sausage and egg favorite, refried beans, or some other concoction. I remember Mama carefully wrapping them in waxed paper before filling the Thermos with hot coffee.

When Papa returned from his carpenter's job, I wiped off the sawdust before opening the lunch pail. There I often found the *"taco paseado."* Mama called it the traveled taco because it left with Papa in the morning and returned at the end of the day.

Papa usually tucked a surprise for us in there too. Maybe it was a toy forgotten by a careless child, a shiny rock, or a piece of wood he hastily sanded for us. Sometimes he saved an apple or another piece of fruit.

The surprises were fun but it was the taco that enticed my senses. I remember vying with my siblings for the taco but we always shared. It wasn't that we were hungry just that the taco was a real treat.

We heated up Mama's griddle and placed the taco, still wrapped in waxed paper to warm it up. The tortilla would toast to a delicious brown crunch while the aroma of the zesty filling filled the air. We waited anxiously, distracted only by playing with the "surprise."

When the taco was ready we pulled back the melted waxed paper and divided the treat. It was such a simple thing, yet had a delectable taste. Sometimes the lunch pail returned empty and Papa made us laugh when he declared that Mama's delicious taco had been sold for exorbitant amounts.

In an informal study, I asked about the "*taco paseado*" and found that it was common practice in other families. Perhaps it was not called "*taco paseado*" but most respondents remembered savoring the traveled sandwich.

When I was a young bride my father-in-law laughed at my delight to find a "*taco paseado*" in his lunch pail. It made me wonder if our Mamas didn't pack an extra taco for their children to enjoy.

The memory of Papa bringing small tokens to remind us that he was thinking about his kids while he worked is etched in my mind.

Those tangible surprises are all gone except for the old horseshoe hanging above the back door, a small memento of a father's love for an impressionable daughter.

April 1997

Comjim and the Whitman Chocolates Box

◆

A shiny tin box of Whitman Candies greeted me when I returned from work one day. Whitman Chocolates first introduced the fancy Salmagundi design in 1924. It was a gift from Leonor, my next door neighbor and brought back memories of a childhood neighbor.

Long ago when I was growing up in El Paso's Second Ward, a solitary man lived in the same tenement. I never knew his name but we called him Comjim because after letting the cat, he'd look out the door calling, "Come Jim…" So "Comjim" became his name.

The tenement on South Tays Street was home to many family members. My cousin Sara lived with her parents in apartment number one and we were tucked in between. We had wonderful times together, sharing holidays and building memories. My cousins and I played with the same toys and sometimes quarreled over whose turn it was to ride the one bicycle in our midst. Sara was my best friend, and because she was older, I regarded her as the older sister I pined for.

One day while we played in the dusty yard, Comjim slipped a Whitman Sampler Chocolate box out the door. Sara reached it first and opened it to the rustling of brown wrappers inside. A chocolate aroma tickled my nose and I reached out hoping that a bonbon had been overlooked. But, the box was empty.

In my mind the yellow box offered other possibilities. I saw it as a container for pencils, my rock collection and the jacks and red ball. I wanted it, but Sara possessively opened and closed the hinged lid, reading aloud the diagram printed inside the yellow top.

"Raspberry Crème, Hand Dipped Cherry Cordial, Chocolate Truffle…" Her tongue enunciated every delicious variety on the lid. "Do you smell the chocolate?" She asked.

"Yes, let me have it," I said reaching for the empty box. She pulled it away and clutched it to her chest.

Then the apartment door opened.

"Come, Jim," the man called and the striped yellow cat scampered inside. I caught a glimpse of the apartment and saw newspapers littering the floor as the door closed off my view.

I asked Mama about him but she didn't know where he came from.

"He's a loner, won't talk to anyone," Mama said shaking her head. The other neighbors left him alone but Mama would take hot food, coffee and *pan dulce* covered with a dishtowel, knock and leave the offering outside his door. Later he returned the empty dishes to the same spot and I'd pick them up. Mama felt compassion for him because he was the only *"Americano"* who lived among us.

He died in the apartment one day and his body was taken away by ambulance. Some said money was found stashed in the mattress when another *"Americano"* came to clear his things. Nobody from the tenement attended his funeral and Jim his cat disappeared.

That day, when we found the box, Sara and I both wanted it and I reluctantly let her have it. Years later, I saved every Whitman box to hold valentines, treasured school pictures, and even a few love letters.

My affection for those famous chocolates in the familiar yellow box never wavered. As my kids grew, I hoarded the boxes and urged them to store their treasures in the hinged cartons rather than the smelly cigar boxes recommended by teachers.

January 1997

Bus Ride to
Lifetime Friendship

◆

The other day when the thermometer climbed to 90 degrees I was walking across the street to the Norwest Bank. Suddenly the heel of my shoe sank into the asphalt. The hot sun had softened the pavement into a quicksand consistency that momentarily halted my stride. That reminded me of Anita, a longtime friend who wore bareback high-heeled shoes with a lot of style.

I met the young dark haired beauty on the bus when I was sixteen. Every day when I traveled home from Burges High School, she rode home from her job downtown. Anita was twenty and her stature was commanding.

The popcorn machine at Kress always lured me in and I boarded the bus with a large bag of white puffs ready to share with my friend. She listened as I rambled about school activities and sometimes she offered advice.

The young woman embodied all that I wanted to be. Her long, dark hair glimmered with auburn highlights and the big dark eyes flashed with excitement. Her perfume was so intoxicating that I saved enough lunch money to buy a bottle of "White Shoulders." But it made me sneeze and disappointment stung when the perfume didn't elicit excitement with me.

Anita bought classy hats, chic dresses and shoes that I could never afford. One day I splurged on a wide-brimmed white straw hat with black trim at the White House Millinery Department while trying to imitate her style. She helped me select my graduation dress and gave instructions on how to show off my hair under the mortarboard. Her input gave me confidence as our friendship thrived. She also helped me recognize my own assets and gave me polish.

"You're lucky to be tall, just pull back your shoulders and walk proud," she said when I fretted about my height. Her reassurances helped me overcome an awkward stage.

When I fell in love she recognized the signs and approved of my choice. Anita recommended the Juarez woman who created my wedding dress and counseled me on the details that befuddle young brides. The vision of her dancing at my wedding with the radiant smile of a proud sister is locked in my mind.

Yes, Anita was sophistication in motion but it was her high heels that impressed me. She preferred slings, those high fashioned barebacked shoes that accented sexy ankles and reminded me of Marilyn Monroe.

One day I slipped my size eight tootsies into patent leather slings and headed for the bus stop. As I crossed Mills Street, the hot softened asphalt entrapped my heels and sent me scampering in stocking feet to retrieve my shoes from the middle of the street. The embarrassment made me give up the sexy things and settle for practical footwear.

Anita and I have shared good and bad times and made many wonderful memories along the way. She was my "Big sister" and always will be my very dear friend. I thank God for putting her beside me on the El Paso City Lines bus so long ago.

June 1997

Flash of Fuchsia

◆

As I rushed to an appointment my gaze fell on a pot of blooming geraniums. The bright fuchsia tint made me stop and brought back a memory from the recesses of my mind.

Swimming has always been one of my favorite sports and I recall spending long days in the pool. The summer of my 15th year was almost gone leaving me deeply tanned from the hours spent learning to dive from the high board at Memorial Park.

I returned home and my head was in the refrigerator searching for something to eat when Mama announced a surprise for me. "I know you need a new swim suit," she said, handing me a Popular Dry Goods paper bag.

Inside something was wrapped in white tissue paper. The paper rustled as I pulled it off. It was a bathing suit in the same fuchsia shade as the geraniums that triggered my memory. White piping accented the bodice against the bright color.

"Oh Mama, it's so pretty, thanks," I said rushing off to try it on. Visions of my skinny body drawing admiration were already filling my head.

The next day I was wrapped in a big towel and sauntered toward my friends. Then as casual as you please, I let the towel drop. My friend Lita's jaw dropped.

"Ooh, what a pretty color," she said, and I noticed the other girls staring my way.

A young lifeguard was teaching us the diving techniques. As I climbed the ladder he said, "Remember to keep your head down."

Standing on the high board I felt like an Olympian when I heard him say, "That's a nice new suit." There was a jaunt in my step as I jumped off and hit the water. All day I felt like a million bucks in my new bathing suit.

A few days later I hit the bottom of the pool with my head. I heard my sister Angie scream when I emerged bleeding with a knot on my forehead. Maybe I was showing off too much in the new swimsuit.

I wore the bathing suit until the chlorine faded the bright color into a pale pink and it lost its elasticity. With that piece of colorful material Mama gave me confidence to meet the challenges that lay ahead. It was her encouragement that propelled me to take risks in life.

Times were tough when I was fifteen and with four siblings, money was scarce in our family. I don't know what sacrifices Mama made to buy a swimsuit at the Popular but she sure made me feel special.

That flash of fuchsia geraniums brought back the memory of Mama's way of giving her impressionable daughter confidence. I'll climb that diving board for you any time, Mama. Thank you, I love you.

June 1997

You Must Be a Vampire

◆

While browsing in a gift shop I picked up a ceramic statue of a nun. My fingers traced the rosary beads hanging down the blue habit. Her hands disappeared into the sleeves and a serene face was framed in the traditional white wimple. I laughed aloud remembering a moment locked in my mind.

Mama was hospitalized with an illness that no one discussed with me. Ester, Mama's friend cooked for us and I clung to every word Papa told her about Mama's illness. I heard words like "hemorrhaging" and "anemia" and was afraid Mama was dying.

On the fifth day of her hospital stay, Papa asked me to select an outfit for Mama.

"You and I are going to bring her home." Quickly I threw a dress and personal items for Mama into a grocery sack and rode the bus downtown with him.

At the hospital I flew into her arms but it was clear that Mama was anxious to leave. She said, "Sister says I can't go home until we have donated blood to replace the transfusions I got." She pulled the privacy curtain to change into her clothes.

"Sister is very angry," Mama said coming out smoothing out the wrinkles in her dress. My careless packing embarrassed me and I hung my head but Mama hugged me without a word.

We heard rustling and turned to see the Mother Superior march into the room. Her habit brushed the floor and the wimple encircled her face. Mama introduced us but the woman just glared back.

"This must be paid," she waved a piece of paper. Mama's gaze fell. Sister crossed her arms, unmoved. Mama said, "I need to go home and take care of my family."

"You're not going anywhere until this is taken care of," she fanned the air with the bill. Every good image of nuns was banished from my mind.

"She's going to make Mama stay," I thought.

Papa's jaw clenched but Mama took his hand and held it.

"That's not a problem. I just got paid," Papa said pulling an envelope from his pocket.

The nun hissed, "I don't want money, I want the blood."

Papa's brown eyes flashed and his fists balled up. He stepped away from Mama and into the nun's face.

"Then you must be a vampire." He blurted.

The nun's face suddenly looked pinched in the wimple. "You…can't talk…but…but" she stammered. They stood face to face, exchanging angry glares. Then sister gathered her skirt and stormed out of the room.

Mama put her things in the paper sack and we walked to the front office where Papa paid the bill.

"Don't worry, I'll get my friends to donate blood to pay for the transfusions. I don't want that vampire to come after us." Papa said loudly.

Outside Papa announced we were going to celebrate. My folks exchanged loving glances over lunch and didn't talk about the incident. I was just glad that Mama was going home and reveled in their love.

I'm not sure if we celebrated my mother's release or the way Papa dealt with the situation. They never spoke about the confrontation and it was buried in my mind until that day in the gift shop.

Papa's friends and brothers donated enough pints to replenish the blood bank. Sister's hospital fell into financial ruin before she left town. I bought the ceramic nun and placed it on the piano as a reminder of Papa's wit and his triumph in an uncharitable moment.

June 1997

Monsters that Lurked
at the Theater

◆

As I walked past the Plaza Theater my mind filled with memories of summer vacations when movies were our main entertainment. Twinkling stars in the dark ceiling were hypnotic and music from the calliope filled the air.

Frankenstein, Dracula and the Mummy made us scream but we returned for more. During spring holiday, "The Greatest Story Ever Told" lured everybody and we waited in the long line around the White House Department Store. A can of food was the admission price that helped us understand compassion for the less fortunate.

"The Thing," was playing on my birthday and while I bought tickets my little brother started to cry. "The Thing's" mangled hand creeping bloodily on the poster behind the glass scared him. It ruined my day because instead of watching "The Thing," we saw "Snow White and the Seven Dwarfs."

As a teenager I attended a midnight show at the Plaza with my cousins. Having a bunch of cousins was like having a multitude of best friends as we trekked Downtown for the midnight show.

The entertainment started with a magic show where the magician called for volunteers. I jumped at the chance to sit on stage to watch the magician perform sleight of hand tricks and produce birds from thin air.

The magic maker asked a young man sitting beside me if he'd ever been scared out of his pants. As they bantered back and forth I noticed the light shining on the wires attached to the rivets on the young man's pants. The wires led somewhere behind the curtain.

"You wouldn't be scared if Dracula showed up?" The magician feigned disbelief. Frightening screams rose as bats flew in all directions. They swooped into the ivy-covered trellises beneath the stars. In a whirl of cape, Dracula appeared on stage, incisors gleaming in his pasty face.

I froze in my chair as the vampire looked at me but at that moment the guy who wasn't scared jumped back. Dracula whirled to face him and suddenly the blue jeans were literally pulled from his body. As quickly as he had appeared Dracula jumped from the stage and disappeared as the audience cringed in their seats.

The young man stood shaking in polka-dotted briefs as the crowd roared. The fellow hid behind his hands until the magician produced a multicolored scarf. Giggling girls pointed as the hairy-legged man covered himself and ran backstage. But I knew the wires behind the curtain pulled off his pants.

Suddenly a weight rested on my shoulder and turning, my eyes lifted a long length into the face of Frankenstein. A scream escaped from my mouth and I fled the stage, jumping over the orchestra pit, up the aisle and out of the theater.

My cousin Junior found me across the street hugging the historical tree that served pioneer El Paso as a newspaper. Newsworthy items were hung on that old tree but now it was dear life I was clinging to. Tears streaked my face but nothing would make me let go.

"Come on, we're missing the show," Junior said but I wouldn't go back in. A police officer stopped by and when he heard about Frankenstein chuckled without compassion. Junior went back in and the uniformed man stayed with me until the midnight crowd came out.

"Ooh, you chickened out." Their teasing hurt but I endured it silently. It wasn't their shoulder Franky touched, and besides the musty smell of his clothes still filled my nose.

It was a long time before I could attend another scary movie. Then Hitchcock made "Psycho." But that's another story.

June 1997

Estropajos or *Puffs*

◆

On special occasions my kids are generous with cards and presents. One of those gifts was a basket filled with bath toiletries that promised skin rejuvenation. A fluffy white puff was wrapped around a bottle of liquid body gel. You know the kind, they come in a variety of colors and brands.

It reminded me of an *estropajo*, the puff of my youth. That "*estropajo*" or scrubber was made from cactus fiber and rolled into a circle or folded in a square resembling today's natural loufa.

Mama bought *estropajos* in Juarez and everybody used them. I spotted them in Abuelita's house, Tia Luz's bathroom and in my best friend's shower stall. When the *estropajo* was new, it was rough, but after a while it softened with use.

After we played in the dusty yard Mama scrubbed us with the *estropajo* until our skin shined. I always wanted to be the last one in the tub, knowing the *estropajo* had softened when my turn came around. After long use, the *estropajo* became stringy and fell apart but Mama would bring out a new one.

Recently I poured liquid body gel and filled the tub with frothy suds that permeated the air with a delicate fragrance. I slipped in and allowed the water to bathe away the stress of the day. A scented candle tossed flickering patterns against the wall just before I closed my eyes behind the gel-filled pink masque. An inflatable pillow included in the gift basket supported my neck.

I remember when I craved a little spare time for a long bath. With four young children it seemed that my hair was always in the ugly spongy curlers that preceded blow dryers. It was hard to find time between chores to take out the pink sponges and brush out my hair. Home movies and photographs captured me folding laundry or in unflattering times that make our kids laugh. Luxuriating baths, not quite. Five-minute showers became my style.

Now the children who kept me from indulging in fragrant tubs bring me aromatic gifts with promises of youthful skin. Yet a quick shower still fits my schedule and the ecology.

It's true, the more things change, the more they remain the same. The new synthetic scrubbers in pink, green, and lilac hues are fast replacing the wash cloth. There on the store shelf, you'll find the puff, the body buff and the mitt next to the loufa and even a scrub glove. They serve the same purpose as the *estropajo*. But now Dove, Ivory and Oil of Olay include the "puffs" free with the purchase of a new "body wash."

Oil of Olay had promised renewed skin but all I got was a relaxing bath and water wrinkles. Trying to work out a crossword puzzle proved too challenging with the light of the flickering candle.

The puffs have become as common as *the estropajos* were for me. The next time I go to Juarez, I'm going to search for an *estropajo*. I'm curious to see how the cactus "puff" compares with the its modern counterpart.

May 1997

El Tranvia

———————— ◆ ————————

On a recent trip to Juarez my eye fell on the remnants of rail tracks that once served the old trolley. Today's rubber-wheeled trolleys are fine but they lack the charm of the antique cars that hummed with electricity as the bell clanged to announce its arrival. In those days, the trolley ferried people back and forth across the international bridge.

My pace slackened as memories flooded my mind. I often accompanied Mama to Juarez to buy groceries. First she exchanged dollars at the rate of 12 to 1 at the *Casa de Cambio* while Mariachi music filtered out from the San Luis Bar next door. I asked Mama if we could drop in to hear them but she refused. Then I got a lecture about going into such places.

At *Abarrotes La Morenita,* the loquacious Chinese grocery owner always inquired about my schoolwork. In flawless Spanish, he stressed the importance of education. At the rear counter Mama ordered two kilos of bola and the butcher wrapped up sirloin steak in sparkling white paper.

Next we went to *La Florida* where Mama bought unrefined sugar and coffee. She picked limes, cilantro and ordered avocados without pits at the market near the cathedral.

Sliced jicama sprinkled with red chili powder and peeled red *"tunas"* were prominent at the market. While Mama selected vegetables I relished a prickly pear whose red juice stained my lips brighter than lipstick.

For the return trip we waited for the *"tranvia"* in front of a photo studio where images of bridal couples were frozen in eternal bliss.

Mama looked over the *"cancioneros"* at a newsstand nearby and later Papa sang romantic ballads from the songbook and strummed the guitar.

I watched people produce passports and tattered birth certificates that inspectors scrutinized at the border station. They peered into grocery bags asking, "What are you bringing back from Mexico?" When my turn came, I declared, "American citizen," with genuine pride.

Once we had barely cleared the inspection point when someone's sweet grandmother retrieved a parrot from her large purse. She stroked the groggy bird awake and said she gave him tequila to keep him quiet. *"Asi los paso muy seguido,"* the woman bragged that she smuggled drunken birds often.

Bolting back to reality and the purpose of my recent trip across the bridge I bought a bottle of Bacardi Rum and a box of assorted cookies on my way back.

At the flag poles I paused to look upon the Rio Grande where beggars once stood in murky water waving makeshift cones stuck to long poles. I remember when tourists tossed money while beggars vied to catch the coins with their ingenious contraptions.

Back on the American side I declared my citizenship and paid tax on the liquor. I stood swaying from a strap in the crowded modern trolley. A man sat hugging a liquor bottle. The irony made me smile as I juggled my own package.

The trip took only an hour but it felt like decades into the past. The rum and cookies were as heavy as the memories crowding in my mind. Mariachi music rang in my ears but now it came from a boom-box of a passing low-rider. I was back home.

April 1997

A Flood of Memory

───────────── ◆ ─────────────

The recent floods reminded me of a stormy summer when floods coursed down the Franklin Mountains in the 1950s. Homes in new developments in the Northeast still smelled of fresh paint and the grass in sandy yards was just beginning to take root. Then the rain came as sudden and unpredictable as El Paso rain can be.

The new developments were not designed with proper drainage and runoff from the mountain turned streets into asphalt-bed rivers. When the water receded, the grass sprouting on our roped-off yard was washed away. The neighbor's lawn furniture bore muddy tracks of water. Papa looked at the erosion and said, "At least the rain didn't flood the house, we can always plant new grass."

For several days the rain continued and soldiers from Fort Bliss were called out to fill sandbags. Then they drove around like good Samaritans in fatigues passing them out to people stranded in their homes. The prospect of having to use them terrified us. We looked to the sky hoping the sun would evaporate the clouds but the dark masses gathered angrily and dumped more water.

A military bus ferried people to work because public transportation was halted and many cars were damaged in streets dotted with potholes. Adventuresome kids paddled a canoe down the creek…er, street while pedestrians tried to negotiate the knee-deep water on Mount Shasta Street. To this day Mount Shasta still floods, just not so bad.

When we ran out of milk, Papa and I went to the store. Papa said we must put our faith in God but he checked under the hood before maneuvering our '50 Dodge out into the street. Mama stood at the door watching and probably said a prayer as we drove away.

We drove down Diana Drive and the water was running from curb to curb. Papa drove slowly and explained that it was important not to splash and wet the points inside the distributor cap, which could cause the car to stall. He grumbled when a "smart aleck" sped by and splashed us with a "rooster tail." Later Papa smiled when we saw the speedster idled by "wet points" a short distance ahead.

On the way to Kay's convenience store (later renamed Circle-K) on Dyer and Hercules, we saw beleaguered residents desperately working to keep the water out of their homes. We bought enough milk for a week and on the way out, Papa complained that the milk was more expensive than at Safeway but he didn't want to risk going that far.

We headed home passing cars standing at odd angles because the wheels were buried in chuckholes beneath the water. Two blocks from our house a new Cadillac was idle with a fin pointing toward the sky. Papa said with a touch of bravado, "See, my little Dodge did better than that fancy car."

We prayed for the weather to clear but the rain kept pouring down. Every time it clouded up my brothers made sure that we had enough sand bags on the porch. Newspaper and television reports showed the devastation left by floodwaters and residents clamored for flood relief. My brothers just kept check on the sandbags, as if they were some kind of insurance policy.

Other neighborhoods throughout the city experienced flooding and, unfortunately, some still do today. Northeast residents banded to petition the city to control the flooding and a hasty plan created the drainage ditch between the divided lanes on Diana Drive a few years later.

There's beauty in the Franklin Mountains when the rain seems to paint them green. But there's a lot of empathy for those folks who contend with flooding anywhere. The Diana Ditch yawns empty on sunny days but it functions well to carry the runoff from the mountains away from people's homes.

September 1997

The Banana-Peddling Philospher

◆

John Lucas, a street philosopher, lingers in my mind as one of the many people who added to El Paso's unique character.

His horse-drawn cart laden with bananas meandered along El Paso streets before supermarkets became dots on street corners. The horse lazily moved into the barrio as the aroma of ripe bananas filled the air. A cocky fedora was perched on the horse's mane while red and yellow paper flowers hung limply on either side.

Lucas wrote philosophical words on corrugated cardboard that he displayed on the back of his cart. His words foretold the future and predicted election results.

"The rocket that landed in Juarez was meant for you," he wrote when a missile from White Sands Proving Grounds landed with a loud boom in our sister city of Juarez.

"Raymond Telles will be El Paso's first Mexican mayor," I read during a heated election in the late '50s. It caused my young mind to wonder if his garish painted words indeed revealed a prophet's gift.

In 1964 he peddled bananas at the corner of Campbell and Ninth and his sign predicted, "the Rio Grande will never be the same." President Lyndon Johnson must have seen the sign as his caravan traveled along Ninth Street after he and Mexico's president signed the Chamizal Treaty at the Paso del Norte International Bridge. Sometimes Lucas made citizens smile while others often frowned.

Eager children playing in the barrio streets would beckon mothers who rushed out to place their orders when the banana cart arrived. He would weigh three or four, or maybe just a pair of bananas on the curved tray dangling from the scale on a pole. When he ran out of paper sacks he wrapped the fruit in newspaper. After taking payment, Lucas would throw in an extra banana—"*el pilon*," he called it—sending customers away smiling at his generosity.

Mischievous boys crept up behind the cart to steal bananas while Lucas was busy sacking fruit. They would run away tossing bananas back and forth while the girls giggled from the sidelines. I'm sure Lucas was aware of the pilfering but the street peddler didn't worry about stolen fruit.

John Lucas moved in and out of my life throughout the growing years. I once saw his old horse with the funny hat swatting flies with its tail on Overland Street by the City Market where Lucas apparently picked up his wares. The aging horse pulled the creaking cart along the streets of different neighborhoods. I remember Lucas sold only bananas, though sometimes the fruit was overripe and turning brown. Sales must have been steady for he always returned. When a penniless soul approached, Lucas silently bagged the fruit and gave it away.

I was a teen-ager when I last saw his cart parked curbside on Alameda Street. As the bus sped away I strained my neck but couldn't read the philosophic words he had scribbled on cardboard for all to read.

Lucas and his horse fell victim to the confines of modern safety codes. The horse and cart failed to meet health department requirements and the unique banana peddling came to a halt.

Now when I see street vendors peddling fruit from pickup trucks, I remember John Lucas, the banana philosopher of my youth. With so much going on I wonder what Lucas would have to say about El Paso today.

February 1997

Millie la Negra

◆

I was fourteen and talked the neighborhood grocer into letting me work in his store. Every morning for the first week of summer vacation I volunteered to push the broom and dust the food cans on the shelves.

Then he began paying me a dollar a week for doing the chores. The spending cash was an incentive that helped me get up early, gobble down breakfast, and walk across the street to my "job." Amor's Grocery was named after the owner's romantic surname; Love, and I thoroughly enjoyed the work that summer.

The boys in the hood congregated on the store steps. They talked, laughed and heckled people passing by. The rambunctious crowd varied in age from twelve-year old wanna-bes to older teenagers. They constantly combed their ducktail hairdos and walked with a chip on their shoulders. *"El Wino"* was the leader and notorious for his obnoxious ways.

One day, after sweeping out the store I went outside to continue on the steps. The wild bunch moved aside to let me work. I was intent on the chore when their cackling made me stop.

Looking up I spotted *Millie La Negra,* a neighbor walking saucily towards the store. Thin white material covered her ample breasts jiggling with every step. A wide black belt accented her small waist and the white sandal straps wrapped around her ankles were sexy. But the gang seemed to be focused only on her breasts.

Millie was the beautiful seventeen-year old child of an interracial marriage. She was tall and her graceful walk drew stares wherever she went. Her bronzed tan was natural and the shimmer of her skin enviable.

The street gang eyed her as the mulatta approached. Their mouths gaped as their eyes bounced with every step that she took.

Millie was in front of them when *El Wino* uttered, *"Con esas me acababa de crear…"* My hand gripped the broom frozen in mid-air and I swallowed hard upon hearing a nervous giggle erupt from the crowd.

Millie stopped in her tracks and her eyes narrowed when she heard the odious remark about suckling on her breasts. In a blur I saw one sandal-clad foot move back and her arm swing around as she landed a hefty blow that knocked *El Wino* on his ass.

"Cabron," she hissed looking down on her flattened foe. Then as calmly as you please Millie walked up the steps and into the store.

El Wino picked himself up slowly rubbing his cheek where Millie's fingers left their mark. He was speechless despite the raucous laughter and ridicule from his buddies. I quickly busied myself with the broom again.

When Millie exited I expected more trouble. Her eyes swept over the quiet crowd and she held her head high as she sauntered past. *El Wino's* tattooed fingers hid his eyes and his cohorts glanced away without uttering a word. Her bold action had made quite an impression.

Millie's handling of the situation made me proud. In the past she had endured lecherous looks and snide remarks but not on that summer day. With an instantaneous response she silenced the hooligan and left the memory etched in my mind.

I often wonder what happened to Millie and envision her leading the charge of some world crusade. I see her beguiling and beautiful yet strong and sensitive, remembering a lesson she taught the punk with one mighty blow.

June 1995

Snapshots of Life

◆

Mama's camera has been the window of our lives. With a vintage Brownie she began snapping candid shots of loved ones at different stages of our lives and captured images of relatives we otherwise would never know. The years passed while Mama carefully compiled photo albums for the family.

Last summer my 76-year-old mother watched the opening ceremonies of the 1996 Olympic Games on television and was impressed with the splendor and the athletes. When the Stars and Stripes rose to the tune of the National Anthem, Mama's eyes glistened.

She heard President Clinton welcome the world to Georgia on behalf of all Americans. Spontaneously Mama reached across the end table, picked up her camera and snapped a picture.

Mama tried to identify the young athlete sprint the final lap into the stadium with the Olympic torch held aloft and smiled when a cheering crowd greeted Janet Evans. A brief hush descended when Evans took the final steps and handed the torch to Mohammed Ali.

Instinctively Mama aimed her camera to capture the Great One's gallant effort to ignite the Olympic flame. I suspect that Mama longed to witness that poignant moment but froze it with her lens instead.

In another time and place, she photographed me at age four dressed in a velvet dress, shiny shoes and my hair in Shirley Temple curls. Another snapshot shows a group of neighborhood children; some disheveled while others are spiffy and smiling. Mama made everyone feel special and never excluded anyone in her photos.

Our family story unfolds with black and white photographs, later complemented by color film. With glued corners Mama affixed the time-yellowed images in the pages of our scrapbook.

That pictorial history matches the memories buried in the recesses of my mind. I remember Papa toting a metal lunch box that often contained small surprises for us when he returned at the end of the day. In the photo album, there's a picture of Papa's lunch pail shot from the ground with me standing in the background. Mama's camera preserved the memory for her impressionable girl.

When we lived near the old Bowie High School, Mama often had us pose on cement benches that dotted the campus. In one shot, my brothers and I appear solemn but our Easter outfits are fetching as we crowd onto the hard bench.

During World War II Papa came home on furlough and Mama assembled everybody on the field next to the school. There's Papa standing proud in his uniform with my brother clinging on one side and Grandmother on the other.

When I saw Mama's Olympics photographs snapped right off the television screen, it made me smile. I know if she had been in Atlanta, her photographer's eye would have captured special images to add to the family book.

Those album pages speak volumes of love. Preserved throughout the years, the photos give us a glimpse of the past. Thank you, Mama, for a truly priceless gift.

December 1996

A Trek of Faith

◆

A brilliant sunset colored the sky as I drove past Mount *Cristo Rey* the other day. The walking trail zigzagged like a scar across the mountain. The giant statue of Christ, bathed in golden light evoked a silent prayer.

Cristo Rey has special meaning for me. I remember Mama telling the story of her promise to make a pilgrimage if Papa came home safe from the war. When he returned, they trekked up the mountain to fulfill her promise. Papa carried my toddler brother and joked that the child was heavier than the load he carried in the battle for Malinta Hill.

Corpus Christi Sunday is the day for the pilgrimage. Catholics climb Mount *Cristo Rey* with the bishop leading the faithful in prayer and song. Faithful pilgrims numbering in thousands walk the trail, some barefoot and others on their knees. I remember a man on crutches who picked his way slowly but made it all the way.

As a teenager, I hiked up with *Las Hijas de Maria* from St. Francis Xavier Church. We were rambunctious daughters of Mary who loved rock and roll but focused on the mysteries of the rosary as we meandered up the rugged path. But on the way down, we laughed and talked about boys, out of the earshot of Father Diego, of course.

When I was headed overseas to join my Army husband, my friend made a promise to take me to *Cristo Rey*. Rosemary, her sister Mary Helen, my sister Angie and I made the pilgrimage alone but I wouldn't advise that now. On our return a few years later, we scaled the mountain in thanksgiving for our bouncing baby. My friend's gesture truly touched my heart.

Members of the University of Texas at El Paso track team were seen running up the mountain during training. I remembered a Kenyan native who left us in the dust as he sprinted up the path.

Then there was my friend Lety who traveled from Tucson to make the pilgrimage on a balmy Sunday in October. We stashed our purses in my car trunk and hiked up and down in record time. At the parking lot we said goodbye and Lety drove back to Tucson as we headed home. In Deming, N.M. she remembered that her purse was still secure in my car. I returned it by Greyhound the next day.

Last year we made the climb early, trying to avoid the heat. Near the top two U. S. Border Patrolmen rested on all-terrain motorbikes. They smiled and posed when I snapped their picture. Behind them, a man gingerly picked his way up from the Mexican side toting a crate of oranges to sell to thirsty climbers. His dexterity was impressive since no footpath is available on his side of the rocky peak.

Dancing *Matachines*, a style derived from the *Yaqui* Indians, gathered in a crevice in the granite. The red costumed men and women formed two lines and performed a series of steps to the beat of drums. Beaded dangles on their costumes flashed in the sun. *Matachines* have been called "Soldiers of the Virgin" and their dancing added color to the solemn event.

Reaching the crown around the giant cross we knelt in prayer surrounded by some whose unabashed tears flowed. I photographed the Christ's outstretched arms and felt peaceful in His embrace.

How fortunate for the El Paso region that Father Lourdes Costa had such a wonderful vision. He persuaded his Spanish compatriot Urbici Soler, a gifted sculptor to come and bring his vision to life. *Cristo Rey* remains a spiritual gift that beckons pilgrims from around the world.

July 1997

Pig Headed Tamales

◆

It was bound to happen; after years of joking about it, it was just bound to happen. My sister Angie and I keep the Mexican tradition of making tamales for Christmas and every year when her family travels to El Paso for the holidays we set aside a day especially for the *tamaleada*.

Parent's Magazine angered us with an article that derided Mexican-American customs such as piñatas and the use of pigs' heads in making tamales. We canceled our subscriptions and since then have joked about buying a pig's head to make tamales the "real Mexican way" in spite of the article.

Well, it finally happened, but not entirely by our choice. After years of hearing us jest, last year a generous aunt surprised us with a pig's head. There we were armed with the head and confronted with the opportunity to finally realize our "dream."

My husband said we were crazy but my brother-in-law thought it was a great idea. "Finally you're going to make real tamales like my mom's," he said.

I must confess the idea of handling the porker really turned me off.

First we tried washing it in the kitchen sink but it was too big so we toted pot and all to the back yard. Lobo wagged his tail and sniffed around as the garden hose was hooked up. Then Angie shoved the hose into the cavity and out of the pig's head emitted a bloody mess. Lobo saw that, retreated to his doghouse and left us alone.

We scrubbed it diligently before deciding it was clean enough to boil. By that time the kids had nicknamed it Arnold after the pig in the old television series "Green Acres."

An assortment of friends and relatives arrived to partake of the merriment that usually accompanies a *tamaleada.* Everyone pitches in, helping to knead the *masa,* stir the chile, spread the *masa* on the *ojas,* or simply sip *champurrado* and feel like part of the tradition. This time we also bantered about the head destined for the tamales.

Mom's tamale-making experience is invaluable as she oversees the kneading of the *masa,* a critical step to ensure that the dough is light and fluffy. More important, she gives us the moral support so vital in undertaking a *tamaleada.*

This time however, she said she'd never used a pig's head and couldn't offer any advice.

My sister-in-law arrived and we eagerly sought her guidance. I remembered her mother used a pig's head…didn't she?

"Only once or twice," my sister-in-law said. "Mostly she used pork roasts. I don't know anything about pig heads."

That settled it, we were on our own, without advice or recipe for this culinary endeavor.

"How long do you cook it?" we wondered, "An hour, two, four?"

While the pot simmered we basked in the congeniality of the gathering, sipping coffee laced with Amaretto.

Angie wondered if it was done and stabbed the head with a fork. It squirted steam that sent her off to find relief. When the time came to de-bone the head, my trusting sibling didn't notice that I hastily got busy elsewhere so she could tackle the chore alone.

She happily worked at separating the fat into one platter and the meat into another-it was mostly fat. It's a good thing we prepared a pork roast in case we decided to forsake our aunt's gift.

The kids had begun to warm up to the idea of Arnold's contribution to the tamales until Rob mouthed off about the danger of improperly cooked pork. Again they became dubious and, at that point, I could have strangled my first born child.

After the trouble we went through just to put them in touch with our roots, heritage and traditions, their lack of enthusiasm was beginning to smart.

"Humph, just wait until you taste them," I sniffed smugly.

As children we were surrounded by extended kinfolk and this occasion brought back memories of past *tamaleadas*, piñatas, enchiladas and gingerbread boys at *Abuelita's* house.

A special familial feeling was re-kindled as the aroma of tamales and gingerbread mingled with the warmth of family and friends gathered for the traditional feast. It's that sense of belonging-regardless of where their paths may lead-that we want to give our children.

When the first batch of tamales was ready, everyone gathered in the dining room for a taste. It was unanimous: "Our tamales were indescribably delicious."

My son Rob stubbornly hung back but the raves from the table made him sidle up for a taste.

"It's a five star!" he said, imitating a gourmet critic and everyone laughed when I gave him my mother-knows-best smile and a big hug. We had indeed bonded.

The family enjoyed the feast and our children gained a better understanding our culture. In the process of exploring our heritage, our ancestral pride was re-charged, and that is good.

December 1980

Shared Tamale Making Secrets

◆

At eight o'clock in the morning the waiting line for *masa* was already an hour and a half long at La Colonial Tortilla Factory. I took my place with other tamale makers in the parking lot of a favored place for buying tamale dough. To pass the time I decided to visit with people waiting in line with me.

"How many pounds of *masa* do you make?" I asked a chatty Puerto Rican lady who boasted about her acquired Mexican expertise.

"Fifty pounds," she answered eliciting a murmur among the crowd. She claimed that the prepared tamales were frozen until Christmas Eve when the family gathered to cook them.

"Do you make sweet tamales?"

Some said they didn't bother with the sweet *masa*. Others shared recipes that included pecans, raisins and pineapple in the candied tamale. The memory of Grandmother's sweet tamales floated in my mind.

Some women use pork while others prefer beef or chicken. I told them about *Tamales Chilangos,* a Mexico D.F. recipe made with jalapeño slices, Mennonite cheese, Knorr's chicken broth and a sprig of *epazote,* a scarce Mexican spice. They were all interested in the new described flavor.

These women were proud tamale-makers. While most still mix and knead the dough, many prefer the prepared *masa*.

"I make my tamales real big," said a rotund lady.

"Mine have lots of meat," added another.

They average twenty pounds of *masa* for twenty dozen tamales. Some women tackle as much as fifty pounds while others only make five.

Visiting with women who undertake *tamaleadas* was fun. My new acquaintances talked about their recipes and offered advice. A grand-mother-type told about putting three pennies under an inverted cup. "When the water boils the pennies rattle," she said. "When the rattling stops, they're done," she said with a proud look.

Eyebrows raised until another woman piped in. "I don't need any pennies to rattle," she said. "Just stack the tamales around an inverted coffee can, add boiling water and steam for 45 minutes. The secret is in stacking them right."

All the cooks agreed that lining up the tamales is the critical step. Their fellowship encouraged me to talk about past failures. One Christmas my sister and I borrowed a huge restaurant pot assuming it would lessen the work. We stacked twenty dozen tamales and waited. Several hours later some of the tamales were still raw. We took them out and rearranged them in my Salad Master Stainless Steel Dutch Oven. Fifteen minutes later they were done. We obviously had failed that crit-ical stacking step.

After that fiasco we adopted the method of cooking a few dozen at a time in the Dutch Oven.

Each time the waiting line inched forward the crowd rejoiced. I won-dered aloud why we were so anxious to go home and work.

"Because we love homemade tamales." The unanimous reply made everybody laugh.

Finally it was my turn and I exited with 25 pounds of *masa* ready to face the yearly chore. My spirit was charged by the camaraderie of my fellow *tamaleras*. I wished the fearless cooks a Merry Christmas and said, "I'll see you next year."

Driving home I knew theirs would be a happy *tamaleada*.

December 1996

Dia de las Madres

◆

The month of May evokes images of flowery corsages, perfume and moonlight serenades. As a child I remember the 10th of May as a festive day that began with Papa and his friends strolling in the neighborhood "*dando gallo*," bringing musical serenades for mothers.

The voices singing "*Madrecita Querida*" filtered through the open window as gently as the curtains fluttering in the breeze. Sleepily I heard Papa's rich voice harmonizing with fellow musicians as they strummed guitars and played violins. They whispered plans for the next stop and their voices faded as the men walked on to serenade other wives and mothers before sunrise.

Later in the day the women were overheard talking about "*el gallo*" the men presented while smiles lit up their faces. The men usually slept past breakfast after a long night of song. At church, red corsages representing living mothers were displayed proudly while the solemn white flower testified a painful loss.

Children presented their mothers with verses scribbled on construction paper under the watchful eyes of schoolteachers. I remember cutting out pictures of red roses to glue in the center of a paper doily. Mama rewarded me with a hug when I presented my heartfelt gift. I'm sure the mothers of my classmates were just as pleased.

Memories linger as I pause in thanksgiving for a mother who lights up my life with her smile and gentle ways. I remember a card selected before I learned to read. At the drugstore I picked one with a bouquet of yellow roses as Papa tried to persuade me to select another. I was adamant that Mama would like the pretty flowers. On the front the message read. "To a Wonderful Sister." It makes me smile that after all these years Mama still saves that card.

As a teen-ager I sang *"Maria Bonita"* because I thought Papa had written it for Mama. Later I learned that Agustin Lara wrote it for another Maria.

Mama is my friend, my confidant and mentor. Her lessons were imparted by example. She always provided support and encouragement in each new venture. All that I am is owed to that wonderful woman.

The other day I heard an old song that said, "you always hurt the one you love, the one you shouldn't hurt at all. You always break the kindest heart with a hasty word you can't recall."

That's the way it is with mothers, we hurt them but they are always ready to forgive.

I confess to being guilty of blurting out hasty words that I could never take back. Mama's heart of gold deserves more accolades, flowers and gold.

May gives us a chance to shower mothers with love but every other day I strive to show my devotion.

I cook her favorite dishes, take her to a baseball game and give her the things that bring her pleasure. Mama, you are my hero. I hope to be at least half the mother you are.

I love you, Happy Mother's Day.

May 1997

Raspados

———————————— ◆ ————————————

Snow cones those shaved ice concoctions flavored with an assortment of tastes are perfect for cooling off on three-digit summer days. Just thinking about them makes my mouth water.

My grandfather was an industrious man who shaved ice with a hand shaver and sold snow cones on his off time. His white baker clothes were stained with multi-colors of the flavors he sprinkled on the ice. For one of my birthdays I remember Mama baking a cake and making piles of enchiladas for our guests.

"Whoosh, whoosh," the sound rang out as my grandfather shaved ice from a big ice slab. Then he piled the ice flakes into paper cones and asked what flavor we wanted. We relished snow cones in different flavors because it was my special day.

Raspados, as snow cones are called in Spanish are cool refreshments any time but especially welcomed in the summer when El Paso temperatures are scorching. Those ice cream trucks rolling past the neighborhood with warbly tunes emitting from loudspeakers to attract attention also sell snow cones. Unfortunately those *raspados* are frozen solid and lack flavor. I bought one that was tinted red, white and blue but could never figure out what the flavor was.

When our son was playing Little League Baseball we enjoyed snow cones while our might Casey was at bat. Mom, Dad, sisters, and brothers all savored the flavored ice as we urged our tiny team to victory. After the game, we headed for the pizza joint and on the way home bought our little slugger a tasty treat.

Nachita's, a tiny grocery store on Alameda offered great flavors to top the shaved ice. A special treat was to order a scoop of ice cream atop the flavored ice. Those were desserts worth taking a long ride down Alameda Street.

Every neighborhood had a special place that sold *raspados.* Some used flavored evaporated milk. Some had a coconut flavor that was white and left no impression on the ice but awakened your taste buds with a smack. Trips to Juarez gave us a chance to savor unusual tastes like cantaloupe, watermelon and *horchata.* We could also order the flavors in cool drinks that made waiting for the streetcar a pleasant adventure.

A recent television report featured Hawaiian shaved ice that is also offered in El Paso from white Kiosks that spring open during the heat wave. The ice is shaved fine and the list of flavors can make your mouth water.

The television report said that in Hawaii a bean concoction is added at the bottom of the cup before the ice is flavored. I watched faces light up when they tasted the concoction and yearned to travel to Hawaii to try it.

Recently the sun was setting behind the mountains when my husband I stopped for Hawaiian Ice and pondered the long list of enticing offerings. Bubble gum, tiger milk, and coconut joined mango, pineapple, banana, strawberry, and margarita flavors.

I scanned the list and settled on my old, reliable flavor: black cherry. It's like ice cream, I prefer vanilla although I'm called old-fashioned. My children remember that I will consider many flavors but still choose plain, old vanilla.

As the temperature sizzles I savor my black cherry snow cone while other flavors float in my mind. Too bad I can't get a scoop of vanilla ice cream on top.

June 1998

The Bingo Train

---◆---

The Christmas when I was 11 years old there was little money for gifts but fate smiled on me. After catechism class at Saint Ignatius Church the nuns prepared a party for us. They served punch and cookies, we sang Christmas carols and played bingo.

The kind nuns gathered prizes and placed them on the table where we could see them as the game unfolded. A Raggedy Ann doll was slumped against a sack of marbles, a Monopoly game and a box of Chinese Checkers. But it was the toy train with two boxcars that caught my eye.

As the game progressed I placed dry pinto beans on the card and held my breath until the next digit came up. The beans multiplied while I envisioned winning the train to delight my two brothers.

"N-7," sister called out the last number I needed.

"BINGO" I shouted jumping out of my seat.

While the numbers were checked I walked to the gift-laden table. My hand was already on the train when a nun asked. "Don't you want the doll?"

"No, thank you, I want the train."

"Playing jacks with other girls will be fun," the cheerful lady offered with a smile.

My fingers closed around the smooth metal of the train. "I want it for my brothers," I told her.

Her blue eyes softened and a smile lit her face. She nodded and returned the other toys to the table.

My interest in bingo evaporated. I spun the wheels and pushed the boxcar door open and shut. Gobbling down the cookies I fidgeted until we were dismissed.

The sun was peeking through a cloudy sky when I skipped down the steps. On the street I ran all the way home, clutching the prize to my chest.

My brother Chebo was buried in a Superman comic book when I ran in.

"I got a train for your Christmas present," I announced.

Catty rushed in from the next room. His brown eyes widened when the little engine pulled its cargo slowly across the linoleum floor.

Mama asked, "Where did you get it?"

"I won it playing bingo. Sister wanted to give me a rag doll but I wanted the train for Chebo and Catty."

"It's nice that you thought of your brothers," Mama said hugging me close.

There was no room on the small table under our tree for the new toy; instead we watched the engine pull the two boxcars on the bare floor.

The toy provided hours of pleasure before it was gone. Nobody remembers what happened to it but for many years we savored the memory of the joy it gave us. When we gathered for the holidays, the bingo train was remembered.

Last Christmas my husband and I bought an electric train for our grandson and sat on the floor to assemble it. For a long while we watched the tiny headlight glow and laughed when the whistle moaned realistically.

The spell was broken when it was time to get up. Our knees creaked and muscles screamed in pain from the unusual posture.

Finally we wrapped the train in green paper, bound it with red ribbons and waited for the magic to awaken in our grandson's imagination. Someday, he too will build memories that will make him smile in years to come.

December 1996

Frozen Smiles
and Bubble Gum

◆

There's an old photograph in the family album taken by Fine Arts Studio that makes me laugh.

I'm about two years old and dressed in a frilly white dress. Eyes are locked in a stare while my chubby cheeks are rosy and my hair is curled atop my head. My feet are daintily crossed, showing off my shiny cowboy boots as I sit on a stool with a grumpy look.

Mama explained that I didn't smile because as she led me up to the studio, we passed a gumball machine and I asked for some. Mama put the money into the slot and the gum rolled out but I wasn't satisfied. I wanted the whole gumball machine! That's the reason I look so unhappy and K. K. Kazin captured my stern look forever.

Mr. Kazin was a tall man of Mediterranean extraction with a pronounced accent and piercing dark eyes. He served as the official photographer for most El Paso high schools. At some time during our school years many of us posed for graduation pictures, class favorite, football queen and other memorable occasions.

Whenever I was downtown, I would purposely stroll past Fine Arts Studio located in the building between Zale's Jewelry on Texas Street and Lerner's Shop on Mesa and San Antonio to see whose portrait adorned the display window case. It was almost a status symbol to recognize the Mardi Gras Queen from Jefferson High School behind the glass. Invariably, it was the most beautiful girl or the football jock in cap and gown that could be identified.

Mr. Kazin had a knack for making anyone feel special. When I was a cheerleader, he took our pictures for the school yearbook. As he shot individual poses, he elicited my best smile when he said he remembered taking my picture when I was a little girl. Immediately I thought of my grumpy look and the cowboy boots. But he couldn't have remembered and later I decided that this was a way of cajoling great photos from his subjects. His magical work is framed within the pages of time in our family album.

Recently I walked past the studio but instead of photography on Mesa Street, a man was peddling socks at six pair for five bucks and another offered skimpy shorts for $1.99. I searched among stuffed images of Garfield the Cat and T-shirts of the infamous *Chupacabras* for the old display case. There, obscured behind the street vendors was the glass case, adorned with a lacy brassiere and panty set.

Mr. Kazin's camera captured many smiles at exceptional times. His keen eye froze the image of a two year old's temper tantrum and teenager's beaming look. His photographic legacy lays buried in the perfect pictures shelved in yellowed yearbooks in countless El Paso homes.

It saddened me to see the glass that long ago was filled with portraits was now stretched with garish lingerie. I tried to go upstairs to find the studio but another vendor blocked the entrance and the elevator no longer worked.

New fashions are still available at Lerner's but the corner once occupied by Zale's is busy hawking sequined gowns and fake furs. Across the street the Popular had shut its doors for the last time. The familiar display windows that once were draped in elegance now yawned with emptiness.

Finally I went home to flip through the old family album and the pages of old yearbooks to enjoy again the ageless smiles of days gone by.

December 1996

Ben's Tacos

---◆---

I drove away from the downtown area searching for a different place to have lunch and remembered Ben's Tacos. The corner store located at Delta and Park prepares delicious tacos to take out.

After parking the car I walked into the small store and back in time. Green beans, chili con carne and boxes of Faultless Starch were stacked on the shelves behind the counter. But it was the assortment in the display case that caught my eye. Single and double-edged razor blades were stacked next to Red Chief paper pads and yellow pencils. Wooden tops with strings for industrious boys, sacks of marbles, thread in various colors and jacks with red balls for girls beckoned from behind the glass.

I almost laughed out loud remembering the time I bought jacks on an impulse. My friend Dorothy arrived and spotted the toy wrapped in cellophane laying on the table. She challenged me to a game and my husband laughed when I took up the dare. We sat on the kitchen floor and started to play. I bounced the ball and picked up jacks one by one. Then I picked them up by two and had reached six before I missed.

Dorothy was itching to take a turn. She bounced the ball as if she'd never stopped playing and picked up the jacks, one by one, then by pairs, followed by triples and soon the ball flew up and in one swoop, my buddy picked up all ten jacks before the ball touched the floor.

"This old lady's still got it," she boasted when I conceded the game. We giggled like children then labored to get up from the floor.

At Ben's a woman took my order and disappeared into the back of the store. I fetched a bottled soda from the ice chest and sat on the lime-green bench to wait and study the contents in the tiny store. The hot oil sizzled as the tacos were fried and a tempting aroma wafted in the air.

As a kid I remember that Papa would go to Ben's to pick up tacos, some with chile and others without to satisfy his children's tender tongues. The tiny store was always crowded with people waiting while their orders were prepared.

After we married my husband and I left El Paso for a few years and when we came to visit, my mother-in-law would send out for Ben's tacos to satisfy our homesick whim. My father-in-law grumbled that "broasted" chicken from Elmer's was a better treat. He thought it was silly that we would travel hundreds of miles to "eat tiny tacos shells filled with meat and potatoes."

Indeed a potato mixture fills small tortillas but it's the combination of spices and zesty salsa that makes them special. Little did my beloved father-in-law know that those stuffed shells would satisfy connoisseurs for so many years.

The woman returned with a brown paper sack. "*Aqui tiene, una dosena con chile.*" I pocketed the change after paying for my coveted dozen. As I turned for the door, my gaze lingered on the toys behind the glass and I smiled with the memory of two grown women bouncing a red ball on the tiled floor.

At a nearby park I sat under the shade of a tree and opened the grease-stained sack and ate my tacos with gusto. Those tiny tortillas were filled with the same tasty filling and lots of memories.

July 1997

Lizzie in a Sun Bonnet

◆

In the early '50s my grandparents moved from the Second Ward to Logan Heights just outside the city limits and we spent long summers in their home. Nabhan's Grocery at the corner of Broaddus and Dyer and Shapley's on Leavell Street were the only grocers serving the area. We ate pizza at Swanky Franky and bought ice-cream cones at Paul's Café. We also hoarded empty soda bottles to redeem for cash and reveled in our entrepreneurship.

Television was in its infancy showing black-and-white cowboy movies. When "Six Gun Playhouse" was interrupted by fuzzy test patterns, we hiked the mountains and developed a love affair with nature.

The Del Norte Drive-In provided nightly entertainment and charged ten cents for pedestrians. We trekked from Grandmother's house carrying blankets to ward off the evening chill and pillows to cushion our seats on the hard cement benches. There we met neighborhood friends and played on the swings and spun on the merry-go-round until dark when the movie started. During intermission we vied with kids who came with their parents in the family car and crowded into the playground.

Lizzie, an eccentric woman of unknown age, was a daily patron at the theater. Her blue eyes gazed out beneath a sunbonnet secured around her face that left gray strands of hair trailing out. She lived near Burnet School and walked along Dyer Street pulling a red wagon. Full skirts reached her ankles and the old-fashioned bonnet always protected her bowed head. Kids who sometimes taunted her saw a flash of temper but no one really knew her.

Once I got curious and sidled up to peek into the wagon but all I saw were a few empty soda bottles and the dirty blanket she took to the movies. Every evening she came in alone. We wondered if she had a family but no one dared to ask.

Then we became teen-agers and learned to drive. Drive-in theaters were still the rage but now we piled into my father's 1955 Dodge to meet friends at the Del Norte.

One evening as we walked to the snack bar for popcorn I spotted Lizzie sitting on the old cement bench. The sunbonnet was tied around her face long after the sun's descent. Sadness hovered over her bent and aging body. At the playground, the swing hung broken and the merry-go-round was just a memory. Pedestrians no longer were allowed.

According to the latest song, the times they were a changing. Girls wore mini skirts and flashed peace signs while adapting to a changing world. But Lizzie still wore her long skirt and sunbonnet. The red wagon was parked beside her but it was empty. She reminded me of the pioneer women who blazed trails before us. The management allowed her to sit in the pedestrian bench although walk-in traffic was otherwise prohibited.

Lizzie watched movies until the Del Norte Drive-In Theater became history. In my mind I still see her bonnet warding off the sun and the wagon trailing behind. I regret never learning more about the lonely lady in the sunbonnet. The poignant memory of Lizzie at the drive-in makes me long for those carefree days.

January 1997

The Five & Dime Lovers

◆

The young men gathered outside Kress's on Mesa Street, leaning on the fenders of automobiles parked on the curb. At that time the bustling 5-and-10 offered a variety of goods, a lunch counter for quick snacks and a machine that constantly popped the corn that sold a large bag for 10 cents. In the basement, canaries twittered nervously in cages and gold fish glimmered in the aquarium.

The men outside were mostly teen-agers but some seemed a little older. It was hard to tell if they were students but they wore athletic jackets over white t-shirts. Their blue jeans sported folded cuffs and their hair was fashioned in ducktails. They had an aimless appearance; just hanging out, watching the girls go by.

When a woman entered their view, the guys ogled her from head to toe, eyes peeling off her garments until she meandered out of earshot. Then crude comments were made about her. "Wow, did you see how her sweater stretched…?"

Another would reply, "Yeah, but how about her skirt, it was smooth around her derriere…"

Raucous laughter erupted until another distraction came along. As a teenager, my skin rose in goose flesh when I approached the group, their penetrating stares and comments were so unnerving.

My white school sweater with a big purple letter and megaphone outlined in gold caught their attention one fall day. Their glances felt like a thousand fingers tearing at my clothes.

"*Ay mamacita...*" I heard one mutter.

Another voice challenged, "Hey, cheerleader, your team is going to get creamed tonight and you can't help them."

My ears felt hot with the guffaws that followed and my face froze into a dead-ahead stare. Their bravado really stung for my school's football team was already in a winless season. I quickened my pace and fled to catch the bus at San Jacinto Plaza to escape their swaggering bluster. Thereafter I avoided walking past the boisterous men by taking a detour through Franklin's next door. I came out of the store's Oregon Street exit satisfied that a few steps gave me a reprieve.

Nowadays the ghosts of yesterday's Downtown haunt my memory. I remember stopping to admire the diamonds at Hixon's, Zale's, and Feder's. The mannequins in elegant dresses at Glass Apparel, Gilbert's and the White House always enchanted me.

Now vendors selling hair clips, sunglasses and plastic toys beneath the five and ten's ornate architecture block a couple of Kress' doorways. And, before long the building will be vacant.

Across the street Gilbert's fashionable floor space was divided into a makeshift grocery store and a hair-clipping salon. On Mills Street the tiled diamond from Zale's is still embedded in the marble entrance to Arby's Roast Beef.

Looking down on Mesa the Popular Dry Goods Co. boarded empty windows with bright colored murals while at the corner, vegetables and mangoes are offered along with corn tortillas and fresh tomatoes.

City buses still pick up passengers at the plaza but the famous alligators are frozen in an acrylic pose and the merchants of my youth are long gone.

Recalling the bustle of yesterday's Downtown almost makes me yearn for those Kress lover boys leaning against cars who uttered careless comments when girls passed by.

January 1997

Woolworth's End

◆

"Woolworth to close stores across the U.S."

The morning headline was sobering because more than 5,000 employees would be left jobless. After 117 years the five-and-dime where friendly clerks offered personal service will become just a memory. I remember prancing down the entrance steps of the famous 5-and-10 cent store when it was located on Mills Street across the street from the post office.

Whenever we shopped downtown it was a favorite stop. The store offered goods that appealed to young and old. The aisles were stocked with piece goods, notions, cosmetics and toys that triggered the imagination. A lay-away program made it possible to make weekly payments for special purchases without interest charges.

Metal cars and trucks were displayed beside plastic dolls with moving arms and legs and perpetual puckered mouths. Those toys made nifty gifts for boys and girls. After Thanksgiving when the Christmas tree at San Jacinto Plaza was lit we hurried into the store for hot chocolate to ward off the winter cold.

My brother splurged on a wallet that pictured Roy Rogers riding his horse Trigger. Every time we went to the movies he'd pull out the leather billfold to show it off. My cousin ambled over to the counter selling pens that revealed a shapely woman in a bathing suit when it was turned upside down.

The El Paso store had three entrances, one on Mills, another on Mesa Street and a third facing the Texas across from the Popular. A long lunch counter circled around the wall from the Mills entrance to Mesa Street. The polished malt machine and soda dispensers gleamed under the bright lights while vivid illustrations of hamburgers and French fries were placed strategically on the wall. Colored photos of banana splits and chocolate sundaes were mouth-watering temptations.

Mama always treated us to lunch with ice cream dessert after a shopping trip. I liked the club sandwich, and sitting at the counter, we could hear the music being played at the record department across the aisles.

"How much is That Doggie in the Window?" the crooner asked as we sipped ice cream sodas and twirled on the rotating stools. Later we sang along as the song remained on the hit parade for many weeks.

I remember a man who always wore a navy blue sweater with a big white letter and liked to hang out at the record shop. He had a speech impediment but swayed to the music as he hummed along. He sauntered over and asked Mama for a handout.

Mama gave him some change and we watched as he fished out coins from his pocket and tallied them up. Then he returned to the record shop and made a purchase. At the top of the steps he paused, flashed a broad smile and waved goodbye with the latest hit record in his hand.

Bankruptcy is the final blow to 117 years of retailing for F. W. Woolworth where I bought a powder blue sweater with my first paycheck.

The old five-and-dime is another piece of Americana making way for the march of progress. As new retailers take over the personal touch is lost in the shuffle and I'm left with memories that conjure up images that make me smile.

July 1997

La Cuaresma

───────────◆───────────

The Lenten season is a solemn time that stirs my memory. Flyers announcing up-coming missions were distributed after school. Walking home with schoolmates, we chanted, "*Atencion, atencion, todos a la mision.*"

The next week we attended the children's mission but everyone was expected to attend. Missions led by a visiting missionary were tailored for children, young adults and married couples.

I learned lifelong lessons from my best friend's mother, *Doña Rosario*. I loved rock and roll but *Doña Rosario* was so strict, all music was forbidden during Holy Week. Instead we knelt in prayer as she recited the rosary and the litany.

One day I was distracted and uttered by rote; "*Ruega por nosotros, ruega por nosostros.*" Suddenly *Doña Rosario* pinched my arm, just hard enough to bring me back to reality. I wonder if her name gave her a special enthusiasm for the rosary.

Holy Thursdays were spent visiting seven churches where altars and saints were draped in mourning purple and we knelt in private prayer at each stop. Our pilgrimage started at San Francisco Xavier then we walked to Our Lady of the Light on Dolan Street followed by *El Calvario* which was torn down to make way for the freeway. Worshippers of different ages walked the same path and if someone lagged behind, we waited to keep the group together.

The next visit was to Guardian Angel Church, then we hiked up Paisano Drive to Saint Ignatius and stopped at Sacred Heart Church.

Immaculate Conception was next and we ended at Saint Patrick's Cathedral. The pilgrimage helped us reflect on the cross Christ carried to Calvary.

Lenten food is very special. Mama prepared *tortitas de camaron, chacales*, lentils and *capirotada*. The dried corn *chacales* flavored with onions and tomatoes served with fried-shrimp patties in red chile sauce remain my favorite. Those delicacies are happily prepared every year.

Our kids used to frown on *capirotada*, a bread-raisin pudding sweetened with Mexican brown sugar. The funny name also tripped them up but now they eat it with gusto.

On Good Friday we prayed the Stations of the Cross solemnly while the wind howled outside. Good Saturday brought people out to collect a yearly supply of holy water.

During Lent, Mama saved eggshells by making a hole at one end of the eggs she used for breakfast. Before the end of the forty days of *Cuaresma*, Mama stirred food colors in bowls of water and dipped the shells to tint them in pastel shades. While they dried, we helped Mama cut up the Sunday comics into confetti and filled the *cascarones*, spilling colored paper bits on the floor. Then Mama glued a piece of tissue paper over the shell's hole.

Easter Sunday dawned with a visit from the Bunny who left behind the goody basket that Mama had carefully selected. Everybody sported spiffy new clothes and I walked to church in black patent leather shoes. The blooming flowers on the altar were dazzling after the somber purple of the preceding weeks. When the Hallelujahs rose from the choir I joined in and rejoiced.

After church we rushed to crack *cascarones* on unsuspecting heads. Mama and Papa were our first targets and they gamely cooperated. It was a day when no one wanted to be seen without confetti in her hair.

As Lent unfolds, I reflect on the meaning of the season and my faith invigorates me. God sent special people to help mold me along the way. I thank Him for the gift of life.

February 1997

La Doña

◆

One day I was helping my grandmother clear the weeds that threatened to choke her pink Hollyhocks and learned a lesson that remains with me today. I was an inquisitive child who shadowed *Abuelita*, my beloved Grandmother while dispatching a volley of incessant questions.

Abuelita was patiently explaining why the weeds should be removed when a neighbor passed by and extended a customary, "*Buenos dias, Doña Jesusita.*"

My grandmother smiled and returned the wishes for the good day. As the neighbor walked away, I pondered the manner of address-"*Doña*" or "*Don*" is a title of respect in Spanish.

In the barrio the man who sold vegetables was *Don Valentin*, while *Doña Gabriela* had a tinkering piano and it was *Doña Santos* who patted *masa* into delicious corn tortillas that everyone bought. I always found an excuse to visit *Doña Santos* and her grand daughters and she always rewarded me with a tortilla hot off the griddle.

One day I accompanied my uncle to his newspaper job and observed men who tipped their hats and said, *Don Zeferino*, with note of esteem as they passed by. The more familiar *Don Zefe* put a bounce in his step and made him smile.

That long ago day as I watched *Abuelita* pull weeds out of the garden I worried that Doña just didn't have a good ring with Margie. Papa tagged me as his "little Margie" since birth and the more I heard people call out *Doña Maria or Doña Luisa,* the more it worried me that if I ever earned the title, "*Doña Margie*" just wouldn't sound right.

"*Abuelita,* when I'm old, are people going to call me "*Doña Margie?*" I asked. She rose from the weeding chore with a dandelion in hand and a quizzical look in her eye. She discarded the weed, wiped her hands on her apron and put an arm around my shoulders.

"*No hija, no te apures, cuando tu seas grande, te diran "Doña Margarita."* With a smile *Abuelita* said, "Don't worry child, when you grow up you'll be called *Doña Margarita.* She assured me that when the time came, the title of respect would include my given name.

I brooded that "Margie" sounded awkward with "*Doña.*" At that tender age, my heritage had already taught me to address any elder with respect, using *Don, Doña,* or *Señor and Señora* whenever appropriate.

For example, one day my brother and I were sipping ice cream sodas at Gunning Casteel Drug Store downtown while Papa had a prescription filled. I remember we replied "*Si or No Señora*" when the pretty young woman behind the counter asked us questions. After a couple of "*Señoras*" she told us in a stern voice that she was a "*Señorita*" or "Miss" if you please.

Papa and Mama chuckled when he related the story on our return home. That slip of the tongue taught us to address "*Señoras*" as "*Señoritas*" in order to elicit smiles and their good nature.

Now the "*Doña*" stage is dawning in my life and I have reclaimed my given name. It fits better than the moniker Papa gave his little girl. But times have changed and those titles of respect are not often heard. Lamentably the custom has been allowed to escape usage. It's too bad because many "*Dons*" *and Doñas*" have truly earned it.

Perhaps the "*Doña*" may never apply to me but I'll still be Margarita.

March 1997

Guardians of Peace

◆

I drove past Fort Bliss National Cemetery and caught sight of the white tombstones lined up like miniature sentinels on the grassy field. Above them the Stars and Stripes waved gently in the breeze. My mind filled with images of soldiers fighting in foreign lands to guarantee our freedom.

Battles in places with names like Guadacanal, Normandy, Pork Chop Hill, Da Nang and Dhahran were recalled as my mind conjured images of men and women locked in long farewell embraces and loving kisses. I remembered the photos of absent uncles in uniform that hung in my grandparents' living room. Four sons who marched off to fight against the evils of a Nazi madman across the ocean were sorely missed.

As a kid I overheard Papa talk about battles waged in places with names I didn't recognize. I was fifteen when Papa presented me with one of the medals he had been awarded along with a 1945 copy of Yank magazine that told the story of "an excitable Mexican fellow from El Paso, Texas, called the Cisco Kid." According to Yank, my father, Cisco was the first man to reach the top of Malinta Hill, a 280 foot high sheer rock, under which ran the Corregidor tunnels used by the Japanese as headquarters and hospital during the siege of that island from January to May, 1942.

Those soldiers returned from war and were welcomed by a happy nation and tickertape parades. Papa taught us to honor the memory of those that paid the ultimate price and respect the veterans who served. As the colors pass by at every parade, we watched him remove his hat respectfully. We paid homage to those men marching silently on crutches and limping along the road.

But peace was elusive and men went to foreign lands in America's pursuit of democracy and liberty. Their blood spilled on jungle soil, while at home we argued over what was termed an "unjust war." We became a nation divided by ideology, while fathers, husbands, brothers, and sisters suffered on distant shores.

The Stars and Stripes were lowered for the last time in that faraway country. Our soldiers were brought home, leaving behind a string of broken promises of peace. The veterans wounded in limb and spirit were confronted by scornful citizens instead of being welcomed with open arms and words of praise.

"We owe them more than that," I complained but my pleas fell on the deaf ears of those exercising the right to protest what those soldiers fought for.

Americans have always answered the call to bring honor to our nation at every front. Papa still bears the scars from his Malinta Hill climb. The trauma of taking another human life haunts him, and the malaria contracted in the Philippines left him weak. He is a proud veteran who served bravely when his adopted country called, and he has never expressed regret. Younger soldiers are also scarred with haunting nightmares and bewildering illnesses that may have been unleashed in a sandy desert. America enjoys a fragile peace, thanks to God and them.

On Veterans Day I fly the flag in honor of my father and every other soldier who has served our great nation. It's the least I can do for the American men and women who answered the call so that we could enjoy liberty and the pursuit of happiness.

November 1997

Geezer Rockers

◆

A recent story about middle aged musicians got my attention. It referred to the musicians as "geezer rockers." That reminded me that the music makers of my younger days would fit that moniker.

I remember bands that provided music at the CYO, tea dances, sock-hops, proms and football victory dances. We saved our money and waited anxiously as the day approached. Girls didn't need dates, we just went to the dance and waited for the guys standing across the gym to muster enough courage to invite us to dance.

The Rhythmairs were my favorite band because they played songs that fired my soul. They played "Rambunctious," "Kansas City," "Get a Job" and "Night Train" with such aplomb that it sounded like the 78s and 45s that I played on the high fidelity record player.

The band consisted of two saxophones, two guitars, a trumpet, pianist and drums. The musicians doubled up for vocals and for a short while Virgie and Evelyn, two cute girls from El Paso High added a new dimension to the group with a flair for dress and good harmony.

Competition kept the band practicing to excel as the Blue Kings, Night Dreamers, Kingsmen and others whose names I've forgotten vied to be in the top spot.

The Battle of the Bands filled the Coliseum to capacity. Musicians, family members, and fans flocked to the great cattle hall to lend support to their favorite group.

Crinolines, those popular nylon petticoats all the girls wore peeked out from beneath wide skirts as girls jitterbugged to the imitated sounds of Fats Domino and Bill Haley and the Comets. Couples danced cheek-to-cheek when Rhythmairs members Bobby Jackson and Art Wheeler sang melodically for young lovers.

The evening's highlight came when the trophy was awarded to the band voted Number One. The sound of wild cheering bounced off the walls as the bands climbed on stage. Onlookers crowded the dance floor waiting for Father Harold Rahm to make the announcement. A huge trophy was presented and I remember the bronze shining as the winning performers waved the coveted prize above their heads in triumph.

Then the musicians retrieved their instruments and struck up the band while dancers twirled to the rock and roll tunes.

Those young music makers played at weddings and *quincuañeras* with groupies usually in tow. Rusty's on Alameda Street featured rock and roll bands on weekends and became a popular hangout for the younger set.

The years passed and those musicians settled down to raise families. Instruments were packed away while young fathers focused on bringing up babies. When their children joined the school band, the instruments were dusted out of retirement. The musician father now acted as instructor, helping sons with the fingering on the saxophone while nurturing a paternal bond. I married a saxophonist and watched him lovingly guide our sons.

One year I dreamed up the idea to raise money for a worthy cause by reliving those rock and roll days. Fonzie's "Happy Days" was the No. 1 television show and we capitalized on its popularity.

The Rhythmairs, who along the way changed to the Rhythm Heirs agreed to re-group and play for the occasion. We advertised with old photos of the band and their fans packed the Segura-McDonald Hall.

The band began with Quaker City, its signature tune and people boogied onto the floor as though the years had never passed. I heard a silver haired man say, "They're the same guys, just a little heavier and some are bald." He was right, those young men had aged but their music was unmistakable.

We raised a few hundred dollars for the project but the reaction to the Rhythm Heirs proved most heartwarming. For months people commented about the band and the good sounds that the "geezer rockers" still made. When my husband, a former Rhythm Heir pulls out the horn to play those familiar notes, the memory of our teenage years makes me smile.

April 1998

Little Gray Coupe

◆

When I met my husband Bob, he drove a two door customized Chevy coupe. The car was painted pearl gray and glittered in the sun. The tuck and roll upholstery was a popular Juarez job. Bob bought the little coupe with his first earnings and did all the customizing work himself.

He was the first to sport "tiny moon" hubcaps, then replaced them with Fiesta spinners. He installed steel packed mufflers for a throaty sound and kept the white wall tires spotless.

Bob de-chromed the car and removed the door handles for a stream-lined look.

In a recessed headlight he installed an electric control button. My little brother, Chebo was impressed and pushed the button repeatedly until he burned out the solenoid. Bob must've been furious but he kept his cool.

When he left I was afraid I'd lost my boyfriend. He returned a few days later with a new solenoid and brother Chebo kept his mitts off.

Bob ordered lake pipes from J. C. Whitney and painted flames across the hood. He lowered the chassis so the Chevy hugged the ground. The car turned heads everywhere it went

When we married, the Chevy carried us off to happily ever after but Uncle Sam called. I cried and promised to take care of the coupe. On weekends I washed and Chebo waxed it. Once on a quick errand not far from home I had a wreck and totaled the little Chevy. I was afraid to tell Bob but when I did he was only concerned about me. He lamented the end of his pride and joy but assured me that my well being was more important.

Bob was shipped overseas and I saved money to join him. On my arrival a fellow soldier was selling a black 1950 Chevy coupe. I bought the car immediately. It ran well but had nothing on Bob's dream car.

"This replaces my car," Bob said but I knew better.

The snow in Germany piled high but the car never stalled. Bob washed it often but the dirty street slush didn't let it shine. He really tried but the car couldn't replace his little coupe. We drove all over Germany and when we returned stateside we sold for 100 percent profit.

Bob has owned many cars and looks pretty cool driving his red convertible. I spotted a 50 chevy coupe cruising the neighborhood and know it caught Bob's eye. If it's ever for sale I'll be the first in line. It would complete a circle and Bob would keep it humming to the end of its days.

August 1998

Bobby Socks & Poodle Skirts

◆

As a new school year opens I'm reminded of schools days that filled my life with anticipation, trepidation and learning.

Uniforms are now visible on many El Paso campuses but in my day, shopping for clothes was the highlight at the end of summer. The only uniformity was in the white gym clothes we donned for physical education. Plain shorts and shirts with snap buttons for quick dressing were the norm at all schools. The only difference was the name embroidered above the left pocket.

During the summer we'd head downtown and go from store to store looking for long lasting saddle oxfords or penny loafer shoes. I preferred brown loafers but usually had to settle for the black and white oxfords because the construction fit our family budget.

Every girl's wardrobe included poodle skirts and crinolines that rustled as we walked the halls at school. We also had plenty of white bobby socks otherwise we washed them every night. Scarves in various colors were selected to go with sweaters worn with wide circular skirts. Conch and elastic belts that accented tiny waists were quite popular. Multi-colored suede patch-purses were also a critical accessory for stylish coeds.

On the first day of school we strutted in new clothes and shoes and carried three ring binders filled with blank paper ready for class assignments. Teachers doled out book covers donated by various businesses that advertised their products.

By the time the final bell rang we were roasting in heavy clothes too hot for El Paso's Indian summer days. That was before school buildings were air-conditioned and we sweltered as we learned.

When the football season started we bought satin ribbons that assailed the opposing team with sassy messages. We wore ribbons to the pep rallies that fired up our enthusiasm before the game.

We walked to Jones or McKee stadium but sometimes rode with friends. Austin and El Paso were the first schools with football stadiums and the rest of us had to share. Ysleta High in the Lower Valley had its own stadium and a powerhouse team than commanded respect. Camaraderie thrived as we banded to support our team.

Mount Franklin was littered with huge letters proclaiming school pride. Somewhere near the electric star was a giant "B" for Bowie a short distance away an "M" for the Texas Western Miners was whitewashed by engineering students. A large "E" for El Paso was located on the western slope. Nearby a "C" remains not for Coronado but for Cathedral. The eastside of the mountain still bears the "J" for Jefferson but high above on a precarious slope was a huge "B" within a horseshoe for my alma mater Burges High. The "A" for Austin and Irvin's "I" still remain but the others have faded away.

Pride and loyalty ran high between rivals Bowie and Jefferson or El Paso and Austin. The letters on the mountain burned brightly when industrious fellows climbed the slopes to light the diesel or kerosene lamps that gave out a golden glow.

One memorable night the Burges "B" was lit for the first time as our football team struggled to score. The cheerleaders pointed out toward the "B" and horseshoe yelling, "Hey you, look at the shoe." It was the highlight of the night because we went home without scoring a single touchdown.

As students head back to school they are faced with unprecedented pressure. They face a world riddled with conflicting messages about economics, drug use, morality and a world beset with the pollution we leave behind.

Watch out for the eager bright, young faces headed to school, drive with care and wish them a happy journey into the world of learning.

August 1997

Sizzler Contest
Lured Subcribers

◆

As the temperature climbs near 100°, I remember a newspaper competition that awarded prizes to the person who guessed the date and time it would first reach the 100-degree mark.

Entry coupons began appearing in the newspaper as soon as the spring winds disappeared and the temperature began to climb. At home we read the afternoon daily and clipped the entry blank. Then we took turns guessing the day and time for the sizzling temperature.

The competition started with a cash award of $250 and new prizes were added daily. Tickets to the Sun Kings baseball games, radiator service for the car, 50 gallons of gasoline and passes to drive in theaters usually made the list. I remember a crash course in Spanish that was added on the same day that Wholesome Dairy donated 100 gallons of milk. Peyton's ham, bacon, hot dogs and sausage were contributed to appeal to the masses.

When the thermometer reached 100 we rushed to check our list and determine if we were in the running. Invariably it was Mama who guessed the right day but failed to pinpoint the exact time.

We read about the winners whose smiling faces were prominently displayed on the front page. Their willingness to share the long list of merchandise pleased us.

One summer my sister Angie, an admitted chocoholic, collected several blanks hoping to win the boxed chocolates offered by a candy store. My brother wanted the tune-up for his car and I could always use the beauty products.

Diligently we completed the forms and delivered them in batches to the office at Kansas and Mills. Then we monitored Ted Bender's television reports to see if the hot weather would make us winners.

The year Bob and I were married, Mama submitted a coupon specifying the temperature would reach the century mark at 3 p. m. June 10, our wedding day. Wouldn't you know it, at 2:58:44 p.m., the mercury hit the mark. It was probably the very moment our wedding party was toasting to a happy future.

However it was someone else's entry that won with a time closer than Mama's by a minute. I hit the jackpot that day and still contend that the searing temperature was indicative of the intensity of our love and years it would survive.

The Sizzler Contest was an omen of the heat wave. Once the coupons began appearing the temperature climbed steadily. Asphalt streets softened beneath the blazing sun and people scurried to find a shady spot. Women were observed retrieving high-heeled shoes entrapped in the hot tar. After a day of such heat we were sure the magic number had arrived. Besides, the clock at Mutual Savings and Loan misled us with "unofficial temperature quotes." The official 100 mark was confirmed by the reading at the airport. It was as if we had to rely on that government reading to confirm the roasting heat.

Interest in the contest dwindled when the list of prizes began to shrink. Faithful contestants still clipped out the coupons but the contest had lost its appeal. By then my siblings were reading great novels and searching for the Wall Street Journal at the library. It was the Sizzler contest that first snagged our attention with a list of tantalizing prizes but we became avid readers who discovered the world in the printed word. Reading the newspaper still opens up a new field of enjoyment daily, even without a contest.

Now where did I put the crossword puzzle?

June 1998

Marshmallows and Fifty Pounds of Bacon

———————————— ◆ ————————————

"You've just won $100," the announcer said and the winner's excited screams were piercing.

It reminded me of the radio contests I entered so long ago. My friend Renate and I listened to the radio faithfully and dialed the contest number feverishly trying to be the winning caller.

It wasn't easy to do. No sooner did you dial the last digit than the busy signal rang out. Often I'd give up and returned to my housework. The radio was a constant companion as I worked my way through household chores.

"Raindrops keep falling on my head," was a popular refrain that hit the airwaves between announcements for the contest. When I finally got through to the station, it made my day. Then I was disappointed because I wasn't the fourth, sixth of whatever caller they wanted.

After weeks of keeping my ear glued to the radio speaker, I finally won. My prize was a dozen large packages of marshmallows. I'd never seen so many marshmallows outside a grocery store.

After a cookout, we'd roast marshmallows, bring out the Hershey bars and graham crackers and start building S'mores, those delicious, gooey treats learned in Girl Scouts.

Our kids thought they had died and gone to heaven, at least in the beginning. I was always pushing fruit and ice cream for dessert and now broke my own rules and gave them warm, gooey candy packed with chocolate between graham crackers. They basked in their good fortune and relished the S'mores for the first few days.

You know how it is in the summer, the grill is fired up every day. After meat and vegetables I certainly didn't want to waste the red-hot glow of the fire, so we'd roast marshmallows. Besides, twelve packages of marshmallows take up a lot of room and I needed the shelf space. But, who wants to eat marshmallows all the time?

The bags camped out like forgotten pillows in the pantry most of the summer. Any time family gathered for a barbecue I'd bring out the skewers and roast the puffy white candy. We invited the neighbors to partake but after a few times they too began to decline the invitation. The summer was almost over and there were still unopened packages of marshmallows perched on the shelf.

Then I won another prize. Renate and I won generous packages of Peyton's bacon but we had to agree to have our picture in the paper.

Hey, for fifty pounds of bacon, I was willing to have my mug shot featured in their advertisement. I was reminded of that recently when Mama gave me a yellowed piece of paper she clipped out long ago. There was my buddy Renate next to my smiling face among the victors of the Peyton's loot.

Once in a while when I'm rushing home from work, I hear a contest and get the urge to jump into the competition. After all, the prizes are quite enticing-a brand new Volkswagen from Bob Hoy just for naming the Beatles songs, a trip to Disney World, tickets for the De la Hoya Fight, and summer fun at Wet 'n' Wild Water World.

I've outgrown the contest-entering bug. Now I am more selective with my entertainment. Entering contests takes a lot of time and effort and the odds for winning are not good. I'd rather sit by the pool and hear the excited screams of winners who sound like me twenty years ago when winning gave me such a thrill.

Eventually the marshmallows were all gone, the children were glad and I recouped my shelf space.

July 1998

Cheap Date

———————— ◆ ————————

Stories about Americans landing in Juarez jails remind me of a narrow escape. My friend Betty and I dated a couple of fellows who had little money and less common sense. They tried to impress us by taking us to Maxfim's in Juarez, the restaurant of recent notoriety.

On a Sunday afternoon we dashed across the bridge to gas up the car and have it washed. Cars with Texas plates were lined up to buy inexpensive gasoline. Betty and I posed for a picture in front of the car wash. Then we went to the fancy restaurant where a trio strolled among the tables singing and strumming guitars. We ordered from the pricey menu and requested romantic tunes as the tab mounted.

When the bill was presented the fellows announced they didn't have enough money. Betty and I dug into our purses and emptied our pockets but the pooled resources still fell short. The waiters eyed us knowingly as we counted and recounted the money.

I suggested we could "borrow money" from my aunt and uncle who lived a few blocks away. My date and I left the other couple sitting at the table with a promise that we'd hurry back. As we left I thought the pair looked like two pawned puppies waiting for the owner to return.

We reached my uncle's home and I suddenly feared they would be out for a Sunday outing. We were lucky the elderly folks were getting ready for bed. *Tia Mariana* was surprised by our late visit and offered us a cold Pepsi. My uncle asked direct questions and wanted details about what we ate, more importantly, what we drank. I confessed to requesting many songs from the musicians.

"You were gypped but there's no sense arguing," he said sternly and gave us the money to pay up.

"When you get home I know you will tell your mother about this," he admonished. Then he turned to my date and added, "I expect this loan to be paid in a week."

Rushing back to Maxfim's we found our friends sitting in the same spot. The table had been cleared and waiters hovered around them. The place had emptied and the Mariachis were gone. Betty jumped up with relief when she saw us. The bill was settled and as we left, the waiters invited us to come back but I never set foot in that place again.

That night I had a hard time telling Mama about our escapade. I received a tongue lashing for being out late and going to Juarez without permission.

"How could you bother your aunt and uncle?" Mama asked as my conscience gnawed at me. Then she said, "If that young man can't afford to pay he shouldn't be showing off."

The next day the fellow brought the cash to pay off the loan. The experience soured an already shaky relationship and we parted ways.

I had forgotten about him until I read about the problems people create for themselves when they enter foreign lands and violate their laws. The lack of cash could've landed us in the pokey. Thank God my uncle bailed us out, otherwise we would've washed dishes for a long time, or worse.

September 1998

Frozen Delights

◆

The milk tanks at Price's Creameries on Piedras Street caught my eye when the pattern of Holstein cows appeared against the stark white background. From my freeway vantage point I imagined lazy cows chewing cud and eating grass to convert into milk. Then another car cut into my lane and my attention reverted to the traffic.

I remember years ago when my siblings, cousins and I climbed into an uncle's car for a ride to Price's for ice cream cones on hot summer evenings. The ice cream parlor was crowded as we watched the clerk scoop out the flavored cream into double cones. My favorite was vanilla and I savored it down to the very last lick. Sometimes we sat outside and licked the ice cream as it melted in the summer heat. Uncle didn't want spills on the car seats.

Ice cream is my favorite dessert. That must be the reason the Holstein patterns in the distance triggered memories.

Gunning Casteel Drug Stores also featured soda fountains where ice cream sodas, sundaes and banana splits were daily fare. We'd watch the soda fountain attendant split the banana in half and deftly remove the peel before placing it in the glass boat. He piled scoops of vanilla, strawberry and chocolate and added syrup and nuts. A whipped cream mound with a Maraschino cherry was the finishing touch. My eyes always widened when the delectable dessert was placed before me. Sometimes I wondered if I'd finish it but soon I'd be licking the last morsel from the spoon.

Another treat that lingers in mind was the two wafer cookies that held a slice of Neapolitan ice cream between them. Those sandwiches must have been sold elsewhere but I remember the freezer that contained them at Newberry's. When Mama took us shopping we were on our best behavior because our reward was an ice cream sandwich.

Years later we were driving past Newberry's when I spotted the familiar box and asked my husband to stop so I could buy a sandwich. He circled the block and when he returned I had ice cream sandwiches for everyone. Eagerly I peeled off the sticky paper and discovered a soggy wafer. I tried to lick the ice cream but it was freezer burned and lacked the flavor I remembered.

From the back seat a small voice complained, "This ice cream is no good." My son was right. The delightful sandwich was only in my memory.

Then Baskin Robbins with 31 flavors and Dairy Queen with its Dilly bars appeared on the landscape. My favorite dessert now comes in so many flavors it's hard to make a decision.

Red, white, and blue berry from Baskin Robbins suits my patriotic nature and the bubble gum flavor awakens in me the child who blew bubbles that burst onto my face, sticking to my eyelashes. Pralines and cream is delectable next to chocolate mint, but strawberry cheesecake is not far behind.

I admit it, ice cream is my weakness and there was a time when I would sidle up to the Newberry's lunch counter and order a banana split for lunch. Of course that was many pounds ago. Now I'm concerned about cholesterol and reducing the fat in my diet so I take ice cream in tiny doses.

You know how the saying goes, "If it tastes good, it must be bad for you."

So I'll take my chances and indulge with my dose of vanilla. Then there are those cool and tasty snowcones or *raspados*. But that's another column. Pass the ice cream, please.

June 1998

An Officer and Gentleman?

———————— ◆ ————————

The small article was buried in the middle pages of the newspaper but it caught my eye. It reported that the U. S. Navy wouldn't discharge an officer after he mooned a fellow officer. The young man was reported in a joyful state with the decision but my mind was filled with images of bare bottoms invading my space.

Some years ago my husband and I were enjoying a hamburger at Whataburger when a passing car honked for attention. Looking up we were struck by a bare bottom pressed against the car window for the entire world to see. My jaw dropped as the vehicle drove past and laughter from the young people crowded in the car filled the night air.

"Yikes, that takes guts!" I said as other customers giggled. The words were barely out of my mouth when the car turned around and mooned us all again.

Thinking about that reminded me of the streakers who ran across football fields stark naked while the teams huddled. Another one streaked across the diamond while I waited for my team to score during a World Series game. A fearless—and naked—blond woman ran across the stage during the Oscar presentations leaving the narrator speechless. If she wanted to make an impression, she did, but I'm not sure it was a good one. The audience laughed but the young woman faded into the darkness of anonymity.

I could never figure out what triggered people to expose themselves in such a way. Yes, I know Lady Godiva did it on horseback and her notoriety still lives on. But what motivates folks to expose their naked bodies to unexpecting crowds?

After that mooning experience my appetite for the hamburger dissolved. I didn't think that naked bottom pressed against the glass was funny or attractive.

With the return of the Volkswagen Beetle I wonder what antics might return. When the little car first rolled on to the scene, fraternity and sorority members vied to see how many bodies could be packed in the bug.

Another crazy fad had people crowded into a telephone booth by the dozens. I'm sure Guinness has a record just waiting to be broken. Someone is bound to try to pack more bodies into the sleek new model to make it into the famous book of records.

"Don't Look Ethel..." the man pleaded in the song during the streaker rage. When a nude runner appeared we laughed nervously and sighed with relief when the nakedness disappeared

At a local park my children were too busy playing to see the streaker run through.

I still envision the poor man in the song struggling to cover Ethel's eyes as she stretched to look at the naked man.

The military services' commitment to develop young men and women into officer ladies and gentlemen is laudable. Yet the United States Navy ruled to keep the "mooning" officer on active duty despite his childish act. There was nothing gentlemanly about this officer's boorish behavior.

It's just my opinion but I say it takes more courage to maintain your composure than it does to blow it all by dropping your pants.

July 1998

Cotton Picking Labor Day

———————— ◆ ————————

The aroma of grilling hamburgers filled the air and I remembered another Labor Day when I learned the real meaning of labor.

Money was scarce and my brothers and I wanted to earn some cash before summer ended. A cotton field at the end of Hammet Street was ready for picking and presented a perfect job opportunity. We were not deterred by Mama's description of the harsh work.

Very early in the morning Mama packed our lunch and we joined other people walking to the field. The foreman eyed us with hesitation but handed over a canvas sack to fill with the white puffy stuff topping the green plants.

We watched as experienced cotton pickers pulled the cotton from the boll and moved quickly down the row. Then we began picking. My first attempt was successful but a prickly boll stabbed my hand. Stray dry branches scratched my legs and my allergies flared up with the dust. My brothers followed behind and grumbled as we plucked the fluffy cotton from the plants. The sun rose higher as the bag slowly filled up.

My back began to ache, my fingers throbbed and my brothers complained about the labor. But we were determined to finish the job.

Finally we dragged the full bag to be emptied and were disappointed that it weighed so little.

Back in the field we pulled the cotton from the dry bolls as the sun beat down on us. One of our companions sang a mournful love song and then someone else started singing, "*Ay que laureles tan verdes*" As we joined in the feisty song we found renewed energy.

At lunchtime we joined the other workers who sat under the truck's shadow and pulled out our sack lunch. Mama's tortillas filled with chorizo and eggs never tasted so good.

When the foreman flirted with me I gave him one of Mama's tacos. That prompted a burley picker to say "Now you can get away with stuffing rocks in the cotton."

My hands were bleeding and the picking was slow so I cheated a little. The rock fit in my hand and I figured it wouldn't be noticeable when the bag was emptied. My brothers were scared when we approached the truck to empty the bag. Chebo's face was flushed and he stammered, "You're going to get us in trouble."

I watched the needle climb when the bag was hung on the weighing hook. The fruit of my labor spilled and the rock never appeared.

As I returned to work my mouth was dry as cotton. The rest of the afternoon I feared the foreman would come and chase me off the field. The next bag was free of rocks; the extra weight wasn't worth the guilty experience.

By the time the field was cleared our backs ached and our hands were swollen. My brother's face was streaked with sweat and dust. His green eyes flashed when he promised, "I'm never going to do this again. I'm going to college so I'll never have to work in a field."

At home we bathed off the dirt and sweat and rested. Mama rubbed "*Pomada de la Campana*," a soothing salve on our injured hands.

The next day was the first day of my freshman year and as I walked with my friend Tara she asked what I'd done on Labor Day. I stuck out my swollen hands and told her how my brothers and I earned a few dollars picking cotton.

"I guess my hands are hurting so much because I cheated," I said confessing my crime.

That Labor Day lives in my memory as a reminder of how hard some folks still have to work to earn a living. Whenever I wear a cotton garment, I'm thankful that that September day was the only time I labored in a cotton field.

September 1997

Cookies for the Chain Gang

◆

Sheriff's deputies watched the prisoners in coveralls with EPCDF stenciled on the back as they picked up litter. They reminded me of the chain gang that appeared on our street the summer of 1955.

We had moved into a neighborhood in Northeast El Paso and new homeowners were laying sod in the sandy yards. Papa was working, Mama had gone shopping and I was in charge of my siblings.

My brother Catty rode his bike while we baked sugar cookies. Chebo, my other brother read the recipe while I measured ingredients and set the timer on the new range.

As we took out the last batch of cookies, Catty came to report that prisoners were cleaning the street. "They have chains on their ankles and one of them is Nino," he yelled as the screen door slammed behind him.

Nino was a black man from our old neighborhood. We had to investigate.

Six men were sweeping the curb at the corner while armed guards watched. Nino managed an embarrassed smile before hanging his head. We heard the chains around his ankles drag against the pavement when we went back inside.

My sister complained until I promised to give them some of our cookies. "And Kool-Aid too?" she asked between sobs. "Yes, Kool-Aid too."

I went to put the cookies on a platter and mixed the Kool-Aid.

Chebo was indignant when he said, "Nino's not a bad guy."

I stacked a magenta aluminum tumbler into a green one and handed them to Chebo. The ice rattled in the matching pitcher as we headed out the door with our sisters trailing behind.

As we approached Nino, he flashed a smile. Chebo poured the red liquid and our former neighbor guzzled it down. My brother was pouring a second glass when a guard's sudden bellowing froze him.

"What are you doing?" He stalked toward us and snatched the tumbler from Nino tossing it the ground.

"You can't give these criminals anything," he growled.

My brother's eyes flashed, his lips tightened, and a vein in his forehead swelled up. Pulling back his shoulders, he said between clenched teeth, "Do you think we're giving them guns?"

The man's blue eyes stared down into my brother's red face. Chebo put the pitcher down, turned and snatched a cookie from the platter. Whirling back, he broke and held it up to man's face.

"Look it doesn't have anything in it."

We watched my brother, standing 12 years tall, crack the harmless cookies one by one.

"All right, you can take them," the guard grunted and a hint of a smile touched his lips.

The shackled men ate the broken pastries while the guard measured my brother's mettle.

Chebo ordered me to bring more cookies. Suddenly he seemed taller, older and I obeyed. He poured Kool-Aid and glared at the guard.

The prisoners finished the offering, thanked us and continued sweeping the street with the guard strutting behind them. At the end of the block they piled into a truck and drove away.

At dinner we talked about Nino and the chain gang. Papa shook his head while Mama asked God to shine grace upon him.

That was the summer when we learned compassion for people less fortunate than we. But our biggest discovery was that my brother had such inner strength and boundless courage. That baked offering taught lessons that remain with us today.

March 1997

I'll Show You
How to Eat Spaghetti

◆

My husband and I were dining by candlelight in a restaurant where hundreds of wine bottles hanging from the ceiling provide the décor. When a plate of spaghetti was placed before me a flash of memory struck that made me chuckle. Then I had to explain what the mirth was all about.

I was in high school when a young man invited me out for dinner and a movie. He was a college man and a senior at Texas Western College. According to him the ROTC was molding him into an officer and a gentleman as he waited to be commissioned at graduation.

He arrived in a dark suit and a tie that stood out against the crisp white shirt. As we left he assured Mama that we'd be back by 11 p. m.

Gallantly he held the door for me then rushed around to the driver's side. We drove off in his Austin Healy convertible as I secured a scarf around my hair to keep the wind from messing it up. Rudy was an old friend but I didn't consider him a "boyfriend." But he was already in college and that impressed me.

In the Italian restaurant we chatted about our dreams and ambitions. His goal was to be an officer in the Army. I wanted to pursue a degree in psychology.

The waitress took my order for spaghetti and he ordered veal parmigiana with a side of saucy noodles. He fussed with the wine selection but never asked for my opinion. When two glasses and the carafe were set before us, I declined.

"Thanks, but I don't drink." Polite words dripped from my mouth as I pointed out that he should have asked me first. Already the college guy was getting on my nerves.

When my spaghetti plate arrived, Rudy cautioned, "Don't spill any sauce on your pretty dress." I cringed and searched for a retort but smiled instead and said, "Don't worry, I know how to eat spaghetti."

That challenged him and he proceeded to demonstrate how Italians eat the noodles without making a mess.

The college man twirled the fork with fanfare and aimed for his mouth. But the pasta slipped off and dangled from his mouth before dropping on his clothes. His face contorted with horror as he sat with the red mess on his starched shirt and tie. I watched him remove the noodles but the red blotch spread like blood. His face was a picture of embarrassment.

"Try blotching it out, Rudy." I offered my napkin.

His mouth opened and shut before he excused himself and ran off to the men's room. While he was gone I ate the salad, the garlic bread and the spaghetti without spilling any sauce on my "pretty dress."

The waitress stopped by and said, "He won't get it out; it has to be washed." I realized that others had observed his pompous behavior.

Finally he returned but the shirt was wet and still red. Chagrined he said, "It doesn't pay to show off, huh?"

Suddenly I felt much more mature than my date. "Accidents will happen." I said.

He couldn't eat and as we left for the theater I said nobody would notice his shirt in the dark. We watched "Psycho" at the Plaza Theater and I was scared stiff. By the time he took me home, the spaghetti stain on his shirt was the last thing on my mind.

He went on to a career as an officer in the Army. On graduation day he wanted me to pin the bars but instead I rode around in his Austin Healy and arrived late. His mother pinned him and that was probably for the best. He became the officer and gentleman he always wanted to be.

March 1997

Rumbling Trains
and Cinderella

◆

I walked out of the Greater Chamber of Commerce building and felt the ground vibrate beneath my feet. Smoke rose from the Bataan Memorial Trainway as the train passed along the underground rails. The sight and sensation reminded me of the old Crawford Theater. Okay, so I'm dating myself but reminiscing is such fun that I don't mind.

The theater was located on Mesa across the street from San Jacinto Plaza where today cars fill up the parking lot daily. Before the tunnel was built, the railroad tracks on Main Street stopped all traffic in its path. As a kid I remember peering between the wheels at people's legs pacing back and forth as we waited for the train to go by.

The Crawford had two balconies and we often crept up the stairs to spy on young lovers smooching in the dark. A catchy tune preceded the newsreels that provided information from around the world. Previews of coming attractions enticed us to return. Finally the cartoon began and we sat on the edge of our seats with the adventures of Bugs Bunny, Elmer Fudd and P…P…P…Porky Pig.

Sometimes after the movie our folks would treat us to ten-cent hot dogs at the Coney Island. The frankfurters wrapped in steamed buns and topped with chopped cabbage were a favorite treat. Up the street Mac's Delicatessen sold great pastrami sandwiches and kosher pickles. We'd buy the pungent sandwiches and pickles and eat them while we watched Frankenstein movies. The memory of those delicacies makes my mouth water.

As the train meandered along Main Street, smoke from the locomotive filtered into the theater and created strange shadows in the projector light and a yellow hue covered the screen. Yet, the vibrating seats, the diesel smoke and roar of the engine weren't distracting enough to keep us away.

When "Cinderella" showed at the Crawford, our folks allowed us to ride the bus downtown by ourselves to watch the movie. I was charged with the responsibility of watching my brothers and holding the money. When the box office opened we were the first in line.

I proudly bought our tickets and stuffed the change in my pocket. The animated fairy tale was so entertaining that we stayed in our seats as the movie started again and again. With every screening we memorized the dialogue and songs. It was almost dark when we exited the theater and rushed across the street to catch the bus. All the way home we sang the songs from the Disney movie. The memory of Gus-Gus, the fat little mouse singing, "Cinderelly, Cinderelly, clean the kitchen, Cinderelly, Cinderelly" is etched in my mind.

At our bus stop I spotted Mama pacing at the curb. We had caused her great anguish while we watched repeated showings of the film. As soon as we stepped off the bus, Mama began scolding me. I protested and wanted to spread the blame.

"You're the oldest and should have known better," Mama admonished and doled out the punishment. That's one time I regretted being the first-born.

El Paso has come a long way since the railroad arrived. The iron horse's shining rails connected us to the world and remains our link to world trade. Imagine the fuss it must have caused when construction of the tunnel interfered with downtown businesses. Yet, the tunnel sent the train's smoke and rumble underground and made way for modern buildings and parking lots.

As multi-screen theaters debut across our desert landscape I have enjoyed adventure features with surround sound that also make my seat vibrate. Yet there was a certain charm in that old movie house with the double balconies that today's youth will never enjoy.

March 1996

Bomb Shelters in the 'Hood

◆

The other day I saw something that reminded me of bomb shelters. When I was growing up, black and yellow signs were displayed on walls of the library, the courthouse and department stores where the masses could seek shelter in case of a nuclear attack.

One was supposed to seek refuge and expect safe water and food until the danger of radiation passed. At school we watched films in which nuclear blasts began with a mushroom cloud and devastated wide areas. An official-sounding voice advised us to stay clear of the area and "don't drink the water." Bottled water was safe, but in a pinch, water from the ceramic toilet tank was supposed to be safe too.

Today, I still hesitate to put anything in it that might contaminate the water. I don't care if it cleans or deodorizes, I want to save that precious resource.

Thinking about nuclear blasts was frightening. I remember an atomic test broadcast on television. For days Papa rose early to watch the scheduled blast only to be disappointed when it was postponed. Then the test was successful. As I watched the mushroom cloud rise from the earth I wondered if it was worth surviving if the world was leveled and contaminated by radiation.

Papa, my World War II hero, returned home with bad memories but he never built a bomb shelter. One summer the Civil Defense Department conducted practice drills and he sent us to participate "just in case." The wailing sirens of the practice drill at Fort Bliss had an ominous sound that still send chills up my spine. Our neighbors spent thousands of dollars and man-hours building a shelter in the back yard. They stored bottled water, canned food, blankets and flashlights for that fateful day. The kids would talk about the peaches their mother canned and stored in the windowless room.

Ah, but the Cold War ended, thank God. Nuclear war pacts between the feared Russians and good old U.S.A. brought peace and we began to feel safe enough to forget bomb shelters.

The bombs aimed at El Paso from across the ocean became hazy in my mind. I never forgot a target that included Fort Bliss, White Sands and El Paso along with the SAC headquarters and other strategic points in the United States.

In the movie "Red Dawn," Russian and Cuban soldiers invaded America. As young Americans fought against the well-armed invaders my mind filled with images of maps pinpointing strategic regions. Cuba is less than a hundred miles away anything was possible.

The fear of nuclear war was as tangible as the shoe Khrushchev banged on the United Nations table. Now India has declared itself a nuclear power and Pakistan detonated its own lethal weapon while we point fingers and impose sanctions.

It never makes sense when governments spend cold, hard cash while their citizens struggle to eat. The nuclear race is heating up again and the danger is omnipresent.

Many things come back and make me smile; like bell-bottom pants and Nehru jackets but the threat of nuclear war stabs my heart with cold fear.

Nuclear disarmament was not just a catchy phrase; its aim was to avoid wiping out the human race. Let us pray for peace and strive to make it happen.

June 1998

Seinfeld, the Fugitive and M★A★S★H

◆

The hype for the final episode of Seinfeld has been building up for months. Jerry, Elaine, George and Kramer will conclude the show about nothing with millions of fans anxious to see the end. Not that there's anything wrong with that. After all, the show made people laugh over nothing for nine seasons.

It's not the first television program to throw fans into a tizzy because the final chapter is written. Other programs have kept viewers spellbound for weeks on end. Then the final chapter was viewed and reruns began. So what's to lament, repeats will run for at least another ten years.

"The Fugitive" kept me watching every week as he chased the one-armed man, and the Cartwrights riding throughout the Ponderosa made me yearn for trees and streams. The plots were predictable—the doctor would do a good deed and evade the determined flatfoot at the last moment. Meanwhile, Little Joe, Adam, and Hoss gave Pa more gray hairs than he could count. Weekly episodes kept me rooted in my seat as Dr. Kimble searched for the man who left his wife dead and made him the suspect.

The fuss about the final chapter of Seinfeld reminds me of the end of "M★A★S★H." It seemed that the world would end without the antics of drinking doctors and sex-crazed nurses performing surgery in the confines of tents.

My sons were fans of the show, slipping cassettes into the VCR to record every chapter. They watched the weekly serial, the re-runs at five, and when Rob arrived from his night job he watched Hawkeye again. The show captured imaginations with hilarious visions in a faraway war. It was fiction but some people didn't understand that. For them the antics in that make-believe world became real.

For that final "M*A*S*H" episode, my son invited his friends over for a "M*A*S*H Bash." In the front lawn they put up a bivouac tent with a spotlight highlighting whitewashed letters that read "M*A*S*H Lives." As his guests arrived Rob greeted them while wearing combat boots and my terry cloth robe, imitating Hawkeye. He carried a beaker and pitcher of martinis like Hawkeye did when a batch of liquor was cooked up on the show. We cracked up when Tommy arrived as Klinger wrapped up in his mother's shawl and carrying a glittering evening bag. Troy, a big bruiser, was dressed like Hawkeye's buddy, BJ. One by one they came, Radar, Father Mulcahy, Colonel Potter and Hot Lips Hoolihan, a busty blond who was the only female they invited.

They dipped the chips and ate chocolate cake until the show started. They spread out in the living room where Rob had placed another television set, while Bob and I settled in the den. They laughed and carried on but as the show unfolded a silent pall hovered in the room. In the end, Klinger decided to stay behind and the colonel rode Bessie off into the sunset while Hawkeye and BJ said goodbye. It was over. The silence was too much and when I peeked in, the young men struggled to hide their tears. I prayed that this be the only war that they might know.

Seinfield made us laugh at the silliest things. In the beginning Rob said it was a show about nothing and I was amazed that it was true. I'm sure that parties to celebrate and watch the final episode are planned. I've no idea what Kramer will do or what mess George will get into but Elaine will surely be there too. I suspect that Snickers will be served on a plate with a knife and fork to commemorate one episode. Jerry made us see ourselves through the people portrayed on his show. Can we ever forget the soup Nazi? Or the space pen episode?

And so the end is near, just like old Blue Eyes said in a song. But I've laughed; I've cried and had it all. Life goes on. Another show will replace Jerry and we'll hardly miss him because the re-runs will start immediately. Not that there's anything wrong with that.

May 1998

Huesos Locos
and other Sobriquets

◆

Nicknames have always fascinated me. As a kid I envisioned people by their nicknames. I imagined "Tarzan" as the strong man swinging from a tree and "*Betun*" was a neighbor whose dark skin had a shoe polish gloss.

"*Huesos Locos*" was the pretty young girl with the sexy walk. I heard the wolves on the corner whistle and tag her "Crazy Bones" as she passed by.

Papa's friend "*Güero*" played the violin with a flair. That name is given to a blond person or someone with fair skin. I called a colleague whose eyebrows are almost invisible "*Güero*" and had to explain the meaning. Now it makes him chuckle and I know he likes his Spanish moniker. Veronica is a tall, sexy blond who responds with a hearty laugh when I call her "*Güera*."

When young boys got a bad haircut they were usually called "*Pelon*." For example Frank is still called "*Pelon*" although his long black hair is quite attractive. "*Surdo*" was the southpaw who hit the ball out of the field while the diminutive boy was called "*Pichon*" because someone thought he was as fragile as a pigeon. "*Flaco*" was a skinny fellow and many pounds ago someone called me "*Flaca*." The drunkard who staggered home with a bottle of wine in brown paper sack was called "*El Wino*."

The short landlord with thick glasses was called "*Don Hirohito*" but never to his face. "*Chuy*" is a nickname for Jesus whether its namesake is a man or woman. As a kid that confused me because my *Tia Chuy* and *Tio Chuy* were not even related.

Then there are descriptive names like *"Girafa"* for the tall guy who lived on our block. He stared straight ahead and never responded to the name. *"Gordo"* applied to the chubby guy and *"Chapo" or "Chapa"* was given to the short boy or girl.

"El Greñas" was the mophead who became famous for drug dealing and *"Chango"* was a handsome fellow despite the monkey moniker.

"Here comes Liro," someone would say as the short neighbor parked his truck at the curb. "Liro" was short for "Little Man" because that's how it sounded. A friend couldn't recall where the nickname for *"Pitburgo"* came from until someone reminded her that he drove a truck for Pittsburg Glass Company.

"La Tomata" got her nickname because her cheeks were the color of tomatoes when she was a baby. In school she hated the nickname and struggled to shed it. "Nena" got hers because she was the only girl in a family of boys. "Tila's" name was derived from "Gracielita" because her brother couldn't say the diminutive name and "Titi" because her sibling couldn't say sister.

"Chuma" was Jesus Maria and the brother of "Teeny" whose name is Ernestina and "Chalia," short for Rosalia. My best friend Clara was called "Tara" and I envisioned the plantation from "Gone With the Wind."

My brother was called "Chebo" short for Eusebio, and "Tolie" was Eustolia, my friend in school.

"Venado" was Benjamin, a tall good-looking fellow who lived across the street. I always wondered if he got the name because he ran as fast as his namesake, the deer.

Nicknames can be colorful but descriptive names often cause embarrassment. *Flaco, Gordo, Girafa, Chango* have negative connotations but I think Margie, Maggie, Mague and Margo are okay and have responded to all. Just a word of caution if you're considering a sobriquet: they stick for a long time, so be careful what you say.

June 1998

Football Game Blessings

———————— ◆ ————————

I was remembering past Thanksgivings and my mind filled with the simple joys that filled my life while growing up in El Paso.

Those special days when we gathered with relatives at *Abuelita's* house, not just for holidays, but weekly visits when we took long bus rides to her house.

The Turkey Day of my 15th year stands out in my mind. Jefferson High School faced the mighty Bowie Bears in a football match at Jones Stadium. My cousin Sara and I joined schoolmates wrapped in red sweaters with a silver "J" and walked all the way to El Paso High. We sat in the cement bleachers warmed by El Paso's sun and ate roasted pumpkinseeds as we cheered the mighty Foxes.

Alas, our team lost and we saw beleaguered players dejectedly shake hands with the victorious opponents. Then we headed home and the jaunt suddenly seemed longer.

The anticipation of the game that fired our spirits had vanished and the loss weighed heavily on our shoulders as we trudged along. The sun was hiding behind darkening clouds and hunger pains began to grumble in my tummy.

We walked past windows at Luby's Cafeteria and saw patrons enjoying the festive offerings. The aroma emitting from the kitchen teased my senses and urged my pace to quicken.

When we approached Saint Francis Xavier Catholic Church it was suggested we stop to give thanks for our blessings. I shuffled through colored leaves piled around the grotto and grumbled that losing the game was not a blessing. Someone piped in that being able to go to the game was a gift in itself so we walked into the empty church where icons watched us from the altar.

With a sign of the cross I began to pray and ignored my grumbling stomach. I closed my eyes and focused on the gifts bestowed on fifteen years of my life.

Our apartment still smelled of new paint and for the first time I had my own bedroom. Before Sara and I left for the game, Mama had already baked apple pies and a turkey was being stuffed. *Tia* Luz and her family were coming over and we had a new television set.

Above the door in my room, a mini-poster read, "I cried because I had no shoes until I met a man who had no feet." I reflected on that phrase and realized my blessings were numerous and my prayer became more meaningful.

My companions shuffled out of the church and broke my reverie but a grateful spirit had touched my soul. I was quiet as we walked the short distance home.

The aroma of the festive spread welcomed us when Sara and I walked in. Mama had spread a crisp cloth on the table and placed a pumpkin pie in the middle to cool. I waited and reveled in the warmth of my family's circle. It was the moment when I realized the meaning of "my cup runneth over."

Those are the same blessings that touch my heart today. A loving family and a host of friends gathered to share the gifts bestowed upon us.

I've come a long way from that reckless teenager who couldn't see the beauty in tumbling leaves or the gift in the lost football game. I value the time spent with ailing friends and treasure the memories we build from day to day.

I'm grateful to be a daughter, wife, mother, grandmother, sister, and friend. I say, "I love you " to remind loved ones how much I care. With them at my side I can face the world with a smile. So count your blessings today and always and have a happy Thanksgiving Day.

October 1997

Tunas, *Fruit of the Cactus*

◆

Every time I drove past the patch of cactus, the ripe prickly pears caught my eye. The sight reminded me of times when I trailed *Abuelita* behind Skidmore Field near the old Bowie High School in south El Paso. *Abuelita* gingerly plucked the fruit from the *nopales* as if they were strawberries.

I learned the joy of eating *tunas*, as the prickly pears are called in Spanish, by savoring them with my grandmother. She taught me to pick them carefully lest the prickly cactus needles attack my hands.

Papa took us hiking up the foothills of the Franklin Mountains and taught to eat mesquite beans as we discovered nature. The need to implement these survival skills has never arisen but I never forgot them.

I accompanied Mama on shopping trips to Juarez and spotted peeled tunas in a bed of ice in vendor stands. While Mama selected *chile*, tomatoes, and cilantro at the market, I relished a juicy prickly pear and watched people go in and out of Our lady of Guadalupe Church.

My great aunt lived "in the country." Her big adobe house on Kapilowitz Street had a large yard with one cow, some noisy chickens and a great big patch of *nopales*. During a visit the *tunas* were too much for me to resist. While *Abuelita* visited inside I picked a batch, cleaned them and ate to my heart's content.

Doña Feliz, my great aunt, came out and scolded me for eating her *tunas*.

"But you have so many, why worry?" I asked.

My insolent response made her forget the *tunas* and she lit into me for that.

As kids we hiked the foothills of Sugar Loaf Mountain, chasing lizards and jackrabbits. *Abuelita* said she could make candy from cactus. We found a barrel cactus and spent days digging it up with Papa's Army entrenching tool. Later we suffered the pain of needles buried in our hands and legs.

Three days later we pulled the cactus-toting wagon down the hill and *Abuelita* made the candy she promised. I wish I'd paid attention to the recipe but I was too busy plucking out the painful needles.

On a recent day my husband and I drove through the neighborhood and spotted a cactus patch spilling out of a chain-link fence. It was just as alluring as the stubborn cactus we dug out for *Abuelita*. I urged him to stop.

He parked across the street saying he didn't want people to know he was with me. I rang the doorbell to ask if I could pick some *tunas* but no one answered. A neighbor approached and smiled as he went by. I saw that the fence was to keep the cactus out of the concrete drive and decided to pick the fruit without permission.

Birds in nearby trees protested and a mean mocking bird perched on the fence chattered angrily. I was determined to fill the cup with the red fruit despite their protests. Out of the corner of my eye I saw the old Northeast Police Station building and felt a twinge of guilt.

When the cup was full I rose and saw the neighbor returning. He cast an eye at my cup of loot as I hurried to the car.

At home I washed the fruit and chilled it. That evening I sat in the patio relishing the juicy prickly pears while watching the sun set in colorful splendor behind the Franklin Mountains. The seeds reminded me of iron pellets and stains on my fingers were as bright as the red threads on Indian blankets.

My mind filled with wonderful memories of *Abuelita* and Papa who taught me to eat *nopalitos, tunas* and mesquite beans. If I'm ever stranded in the desert, I'm going to have a feast.

September 1998

Christmas Shoeshine Box

◆

Last week as I thought about making, baking and painting gifts, my mind drifted back to the shoeshine box tucked in a corner of our closet. For years that bright orange box has held the polish that makes our shoes shine.

It was Christmas twenty-four years ago when our kids were looking for a special gift for their father that I suggested they make a shoeshine box for him. After all, how hard can it be to put a simple box together?

Across the street a new house was being built and lumber scraps littered the lot. I took the kids over and let them explore the construction site after the workers left. They found nails scattered everywhere and gathered them up as if they were made of gold. Their young minds envisioned many nails in the shoeshine box.

As we headed home with scraps and nails the children chatted about bird and doghouses and other structures. "We'll start tomorrow but we must not tell Dad." I cautioned while tucking them in bed. Then I begin to wonder how the idea would become a reality.

They were depending on me but I was befuddled and didn't know where to start. A search through magazines didn't produce anything that would help us build the shoeshine box. While the project was clear in my mind I couldn't implement it.

Bob worked nights and returned to find me struggling with the idea. I showed him the crude drawing and confessed my dilemma. He chuckled when I mentioned that it was supposed to be a surprise from the kids.

With quick strokes he measured and marked the lumber. Then he took the saw and cut the wood. After that I knew I could guide the children.

The next morning our oldest son's eyes widened when he saw the drawing and fresh cuts on the wooden plank. "Did you do that?" He asked and I let the hanging silence convince him. His sister was equally impressed. I held my youngest son and watched as big brother took the first turn with the saw. Then I helped his sister. All day we struggled to make the teeth cut into the wood. Finally I took the obnoxious tool, made the necessary cut and pretended that they did all the work. When the bottom and sides were ready I let them hammer away.

Soon the scraps took shape with angled sides and a handle. I guided our youngest son's tiny hand as he hammered nails in. When the neighbors stopped to see what the noise was about, the kids puffed up with pride and showed off the crude box.

We found a can of leftover orange paint and they spent the next day covering every inch of bare wood. Then we went shopping for Shinola black and brown polish, brushes, and a buffing rag. The kids stood the brushes on end and arranged the polish neatly in the box.

On Christmas morning our children walked in as their father sipped his first cup of coffee. They tied a green ribbon haphazardly around the box and waited for his reaction.

"Wow, where did this shoeshine box come from?" Bob exclaimed with feigned surprise.

"We made it with wood from across the street," they replied as pride gleamed in their eyes.

"Mom helped us."

Bob and I traded knowing glances.

That gift built by small hands from lumber scraps, nails and all their love is still around, although the bright color makes me push it into the darkest corner of the closet. Now they know the rest of the story.

December 1998

Mama, Gift from the Magi

◆

The Epiphany is approaching with the promise of peace and goodwill toward men. Long ago, gift-bearing Magi found lying in a manger the Christ Child who would give His life to save the world. Around the world the Epiphany is observed in many ways, including filling shoes and stockings with gifts for children.

Seventy-eight years ago another child was born. Mama came into the world on January 6 without fanfare. Her parents were delighted with the youngest daughter who completed their family.

Years later I rushed home to bake a cake for Mama's birthday. As I passed the Queen Anne Bakery the aroma drifting out drew me in. I spotted a white cake with sugar roses arranged in a bouquet in the middle. They represented the real bouquet I couldn't afford, so I paid $4.50 for the cake and rushed to catch the bus.

At 6 o'clock, the vehicle was crowded but I found a seat while others swayed from the straps hanging above me. I held the box on my lap for the ride home. Every time the bus turned I felt the birthday cake slide inside the box and feared that Mama's gift would be squashed.

I felt like the Magi bearing gifts for the infant in Bethlehem. Mama is the angel who brought peace and harmony into our lives. With loving care she reared five children and often did it alone. Papa was an integral part of our lives but was losing his way in a battle with alcoholism that clouded his vision. Mama was always there to guide us with a loving but stern hand that kept us focused.

The ride dragged on as the box weighed on my knees. I balanced it like an acrobat as the vehicle turned and meandered the long way home. When we arrived at my stop I precariously walked up the aisle with the awkward box. Then I walked the last few blocks home.

I couldn't return the friendly wave of neighbors but smiled as I passed by. At the corner John was in the yard tending to his manicured lawn where a late blooming rose survived the cold.

"What's in the box?" he asked.

"A cake for Mama's birthday. It's got red roses like that one." I nodded to the red bloomer.

John immediately snipped the flower off and placed it on top of the cake box.

"Tell your mother 'Happy Birthday' for me."

At home my brothers and sisters were waiting to bake the cake but instead I opened the box to show off the professional pastry. The sides were a little squashed but the roses were still intact. We watched the coffee drip in the glass percolator and when Mama came in we sang the birthday song.

We found a vase for the red rose from the neighbor's yard and told her she deserved a dozen roses from each of us. Her broad smile touched her misty eyes.

"This is more than enough," she said. That's my Mama; no matter what you do, "it's more than enough."

Another year has passed and the day of the Magi is upon us. I found a recipe for *rosca,* the traditional ring cake for this day. I intend to bake and recycle the plastic baby from my daughter-in-law's baby shower into the batter.

Custom dictates that the person who finds the baby in the bread must be host for a party within a month. It's a great way to celebrate Mama's day. I'll buy red roses to make her smile. Happy Birthday Mama. I love you

January 1998

Stolen Kisses in the Cemetery

◆

At a high school reunion I saw a woman with hazel eyes talking excitedly across the room. As usually happens at these events everyone doesn't always recognize everybody else but I remembered details about her that made me smile.

Emily is a vivacious brunette whose sparkling eyes would linger in anyone's mind. In high school her natural beauty and friendly manner drew the boys' attention. As an awkward, gangly teen-ager I yearned to be like her. Her family lived on Yandell Boulevard across from Concordia Cemetery and that was the connection that was etched in my mind.

At Jefferson High School, we shared a class and often huddled in the back of the room to hear Emily describe daring escapades that caused me to dissolve into nervous giggles. She was not allowed to date but would sneak out and meet a beau at the cemetery.

As she talked, my imagination ran wild with vivid images of the pair embracing against the coldness of a granite obelisk. I envisioned the young couple whispering endearments while the moon reflected their entwined silhouettes. Her actions seemed harmless but the thought of lurking in the dark waiting to meet anybody in the cemetery made my skin quiver with goose bumps.

The years slipped by, I moved to another neighborhood and didn't see Emily again. Whenever I drove past the cemetery, I smiled at the thought of that fun-loving girl stealing kisses among broken tombstones in eerie surroundings.

At the school reunion, rock 'n roll music filled the air as I searched for familiar faces. My old friend was spotted twisting the night away ala Chubby Checker. When the music stopped I sought her out.

"After all these years, you remember," Emily squealed with delight.

I blurted out, "Of course I remember, you always met your boyfriend at the cemetery." Her mouth opened and shut, the familiar eyes flashed and she burst out laughing. Tears ran down her face and she held her sides trying to contain the convolutions.

"I hadn't thought about that in ages," Emily stammered. When she regained control, Emily regaled former classmates with the story of the rendezvous at the cemetery. Her husband of many years had heard the story before but seemed to laugh the loudest.

Emily hasn't lost her sense of humor nor has her zest for life diminished.

Her hazel eyes brightened with interest when I mentioned that she probably used John Wesley Hardin's tombstone for a backrest. As an out-of-towner, she was not familiar with the controversy surrounding the gunslinger and the plot where he was buried. I suspect that El Paso has another tourist headed for Concordia Cemetery.

There is something perturbing about cemeteries and the image our minds conjure about burial plots. But didn't Michael Jackson make millions dancing with purported boothill residents in a video labeled "Thriller?"

Graveyards certainly have a wide and strange appeal. Long ago I shivered in my boots when Emily described the innocent kisses stolen with a courageous boy in the darkness of Concordia. When I mentioned my trepidation she said, "the neighbors were very quiet and they never tattled on me."

At the reunion we paused to honor the memory of departed classmates laid to their final rest in serene places. Their tombstones are silent neighbors who never complain and we should respect their peace.

April 1997

Talking with the Angels or Passing Gas?

◆

Our family recently was blessed with the birth of our first grand daughter. The next day I rushed out to buy soft materials in pastel colors and rosebud prints. I hunted for patterns to use in stitching tiny dresses trimmed with lace. Baby girls stir up the urge to sew ruffled frocks and sun suits with matching hats.

The day she came home I held the pink bundle and studied her sleeping face. Her dark hair felt fuzzy against my cheek and her tiny mouth puckered in a delightful way. I introduced myself in those cooing baby sounds unique to grandmothers. In response, Monique Selene's little mouth curled into a smile and as I marveled at God's newest creation, the vision of another tiny bundle filled my mind.

Mama brought home our baby sister swaddled in a pink cloud. We'd been staying with *Abuelita,* our beloved grandmother waiting to meet the new sibling. Mama put the baby in the middle of the big bed and pulled back the flannel blanket. My brothers and I counted her tiny toes and giggled when her little hand encircled my finger.

After our inspection *Abuelita* lifted the tiny bundle and welcomed her home while we gathered around her. The baby rewarded her with a smile and I shouted, "*Abuelita,* she's smiling."

Abuelita responded: "*Se sonrie porque esta platicando con los angelitos.*" She told us the baby was smiling because she was talking with the angels. In my mind, the meeting between the angels and my newborn sister was a joyous event.

Many years later my first child was born in Germany far away from Mama and *Abuelita*. My neighbors were helpful but our conversations were short because they spoke no English. While I was learning to speak German my vocabulary was still limited. When I brought my newborn son home they came to visit and he smiled. I was eager to share *Abuelita's* theory with them. However, their blank expressions revealed my fractured German left them in the dark.

On the baby's first check-up I told the pediatrician about his first smile.

"Oh, he was just passing gas," the Army doctor said, shattering the angelic vision in my mind. Looking from my baby's face into the doctor's eyes I retorted, "I like Grandmother's theory better. She believes that when babies smile they are talking with the angels."

The medicine man gave me a doubtful look with his clinical reply, "That's a nice thought but not likely."

I didn't argue the point but held on to *Abuelita's* theory.

I watched as my new grand daughter slept. She stretched her tiny limbs savoring freedom outside her mother's womb. When she smiled, I knew the angels were telling her about a bright future in this Old World.

Okay, maybe it is an old wives tale. But many grandmothers have passed on the angel theory and it has a lot more charm than the clinical explanation. Besides, this grandmother believes angels communicate with us, we just don't recognize them when they do.

April 1997

Lucky Pennies
and Piggy Banks

◆

The recent peaks and tumbles of the stock market reminded me of old saving habits. Local banks offered an assortment of gifts to encourage saving by clients. Among the enticements I remember: toasters, irons and coin banks of all kinds.

We had a bank that propelled coins into a globe. It entertained us to place nickels and dimes on the rocket, pull back the lever and send the coin sailing in. We also had a round bank that registered every coin inserted in the slot. It was secured with a key that made it hard to "rob the piggy bank."

One of the local banks immortalized school mascots like the Bowie Bear, the El Paso Tiger, the Jefferson Fox, the Austin Panther and the Ysleta Indian with coin banks. An old miner—not Paydirt Pete, but the old Texas Western Miner—filled with copper serves as a bookend on a bookshelf in our home.

Savings and loan institutions encouraged the accumulation of money with folders with slots that held coins. I remember Mama filling the pockets with dimes and quarters. That was an easy way to put change away for a rainy day. I get one of those folders during Lent from our church.

Piggy banks were employed to teach children to save money. My first saving institution was a pink oinker bought in the Juarez Market. Its tail curled up and a red flower was painted on the ham area. I also had a glass Liberty Bell that was first spotted at Kress. I filled it with quarters and put it on display on my dresser.

When our piggy banks were full we emptied them, wrapped the coins up and toted them to the bank. I remember walking into the old State National Bank Building with $10 in rolled coins to open my first bank account.

"Lucky penny pick it up…" that was the beginning of a phrase, repeated when a coin was spotted on the ground. Those stray coins filled a big water jug that is now too heavy to move. People won't bother bending down to pick up the copper. One day a companion grumbled when I stopped to pick up a lost coin. She said she didn't bother picking up anything smaller than a quarter. Not me, I'm still looking for that lucky penny. Besides, bending over is good exercise.

Money under the mattress was never the thing in our home but I remember coins glued to an icon of the Good Samaritan. It was supposed to bring us fortune or something but every time the ice cream truck rolled by I was tempted to pry off the coins to buy my favorite frozen delight.

There's a lot to be said for the practices that encouraged us to put money away for a rainy day. Young men and women dreamed of the first car and saved earnings from the first job to buy it. Now it's usually Mom or Dad who sign for the wheels and often pay the insurance to boot.

There's so much temptation to buy on credit that we forget to save for special things. There was a time when laying away an item was my shopping mode. Those elegant fashions spotted at the Popular and Glass Apparel were laid away with a few dollars down.

W. T. Grant sold coupons that kept Mama on a budget. When all the coupons were torn out of the book, the buying ended.

It was those saving habits learned long ago that built up enough to make the investments that make me titter when the stock market takes a plunge. Maybe it's time to save instead of raising the credit line. That plastic is getting too bulky in my purse.

November 1997

Remedios de la Gente

◆

When allergens threw my friend Connie into a sneezing frenzy I couldn't resist passing on an old remedy. I don't practice medicine but I know what works for me.

Our son was eight years old when allergies made him miserable with the same symptoms. Twice a week we visited the pediatrician who gave him shots and a dose of Benedryl. By the time we returned home, the medication made him drowsy and the poor kid could hardly function to do his homework. One year was especially trying, as my son wouldn't respond to the medication. I gave him the prescribed dosage and watched as his chest expanded but he still struggled to breathe.

Mama suggested I use one of the *remedios de la gente*, a remedy of the people. After all, she nursed our illnesses with home remedies. She gave me dried blossoms from the Mexican Elder tree for a *flor de sauco* brew.

I was skeptical. Dr. Spock's Book on Baby Care had been my bible and it didn't include Mama's old-fashioned home treatments. But watching my son wheeze and struggle to breathe was frustrating and I took Mama's advice.

I boiled water, removed it from the heat and put in a pinch of dried blossoms from the elder tree in Mama's back yard and let it steep. A little honey and lemon juice made it more palatable. When it was cool, Michael drank it and within hours his breathing was almost normal.

That made me a believer. Whenever he started wheezing, I'd brew the tea. Before long we gave up the allergy shots. Michael didn't need them and started playing baseball. B.J. the nurse in the pediatrician's office fussed when we stopped going for his weekly shots. She saw the results in my growing son and perhaps became a believer because she never gave me a hard time after that.

Michael's allergies were relieved with Mama's simple tea. He's grown now but once in a while I still brew the remedy for him.

One day a friend called and complained about her son's allergy. I mentioned *flor de sauco* and gave her brewing instructions. She mixed up the instructions and boiled the blossoms into a bitter tea. Her ailing son complained but drank the brew and found relief despite the bitter taste. Now Selia's a believer too but she avoids boiling the blossoms.

Natural remedies have provided relief for a long time. My grandmother recommended Aloe Vera for pimples that erupted in my adolescent face. Years later my teen-agers almost killed the plant as they found relief for acne problems in my potted succulent.

My uncle used sliced potatoes soaked in vinegar to chase away migraine headaches. I can't vouch for the spuds' effectiveness but he placed the pickled slices on his temples and the mental picture still makes me smile.

Manzanilla or chamomile was such a staple at home that I thought it was a "cure-all." When we lived in Germany I was surprised to find that across the ocean people had as much faith in chamomile as my mother did. *Estafiate* helps sooth acid stomach but requires care in steeping to avoid a bitter taste. Whole cloves relieve toothaches, and *Yerba Buena* is a wonderful mint tea that also will freshen your breath.

Papa recommended Angostura Bitters for frazzled nerves. I guess he learned that remedy from *Abuelita* who kept herbs handy in jelly jars with tight lids.

Now I see herbs displayed with spices in the grocery store. In the drugstore I spotted *Gordolobo* in neat plastic bags along with *flor de sauco*.

Epasote will add flavor to pinto beans and is wonderful in *Tamales Chilangos.* I drink a cinnamon concoction in cold weather and find that an oregano brew relieves coughs from colds.

This is not an endorsement for home remedies. It should also be noted that herbal medicines contain properties that may be harmful. I trust herbal medicine but suspect that it was a dose of Mother's love stirred in the *remedio* that worked magic for me.

November 1997

Afternoon Daily Put to Bed

◆

A bold headline announced the end of the El Paso Herald Post after more than one hundred years of publication. The Scripps-Howard beacon would never shine upon the afternoon daily again.

The Post was delivered at home and I remember Papa reading it while Mama prepared dinner. Then after the kitchen was cleaned up. Mama read the paper and often clipped out recipes that were tucked among the pages of her cookbook.

Then we got to read it. My brothers searched for the sports page while I preferred the society page where the Cotton Queen candidates and Sun Carnival participants flashed broad smiles.

Newspaper boys appeared at street corners Downtown holding out the front page and shouting, "Final, final!" to herald the last edition of the afternoon daily while people hurried home after work. Often, the final edition contained a late-breaking story that didn't appear in the city or home versions of the paper.

I remember a girlfriend from Georgia who moved to El Paso as a young bride with her soldier husband. One day she needed a piece of paper and tried to show off her newly learned Spanish. "Do you have a piece of final?" She asked. I looked bewildered until she said that she had learned the word from boys yelling "Final" at San Jacinto Plaza. We laughed when I explained that it was the "final" edition and not the paper it was printed on that they called out.

The editorial page taught a little history with "It Happened in Old El Paso" by recalling past events. It was a Herald-Post sportswriter who made me angry when he showed favoritism and snubbed my school. That got my attention and I wrote my first letter to the editor to complain.

Soaring temperatures prompted the Sizzler contest sponsored by the Post. We tried to guess the time and date when the temperature would reach 100 degrees and vied to win $200 in cash and donated prizes.

The comics gave us Priscilla's Pop who toted mashed potato sandwiches while saving money to buy his daughter a horse or maybe it was a house. Alley Oop inspired songwriters and Lil Abner loved Daisy Mae but was pursued by Sadie Hawkins. That's a comic strip that would never make it in today's politically correct world but on Sadie Hawkins Day, young women dressed in polka dotted blouses and shorts and paraded on the Texas Western College campus imitating Daisy Mae of comic strip fame. Dick Tracy with his two-way wrist radio was ahead of his time in the fight against crime. All those characters linger in my mind.

There was one tiny item exclusive to the Herald Post that touched my heart. It reported the number of continuous sunny days in El Paso. The tally climbed as old Sol smiled on the region until clouds gathered to obscure its smile. Then the count would start again.

We lived in Germany during my husband's Army stint and I remember the clippings enclosed in letters from home. The sun report was no more than a couple of inches surrounded by shattering news on the front page. That little item brought a little warmth to Germany where we shivered as snow piled up and dark skies obscured the sun.

Through the years the Post became a friend that arrived with thud at the doorstep every afternoon. Sometimes it brought bad news but kept us informed and provided a different view. Courageous reporters wrote stories that brought recognition but sometimes left them ostracized for their inquisitive spirit. All employees deserve our thanks for a job well done. Good luck and God speed.

Yes, the Herald Post was an integral part of El Paso's afternoon life but like a beautiful sunset, it now descends behind an inky horizon to its final rest. That's too bad because the Post was a good friend, it shall be missed.

June 1998

Licking Green, Gold and Royal Stamps

◆

I was surprised to learn that a clock that has been in our family for a long time was obtained with trading stamps. Mama doesn't remember if it was Frontier, Gold Bond, S&H green or Royal Stamps. It doesn't matter; the clock has become a treasured item whose hands bring back special memories.

Trading stamps were given out with every gallon of gasoline and each grocery purchase. Wednesday was double stamp day and Mama returned home with a cache of green or golden stamps. We glued the stamps in the pages and then counted the books as if they were cash. Slick illustrated catalogs listed everything from leather wallets to luggage and television sets. Under the enticing photographs the number of books required to obtain the gifts were listed.

We flipped catalog pages and daydreamed about our wish list. We helped glue the stamps in the books without any commitment to grant our wishes from Mama. One day she surprised me with a Bulova watch. With green stamps she got a pressure cooker and canister set that still occupies space in her kitchen. Plates edged in gold around religious icons were obtained with Gold Bond books and are still stored in the china cabinet.

The fireplace clock that triggered my memory is now a collectible from Master Crafters. A revolving log glows brightly with make-believe fire under the round face.

One Christmas my five year-old sister asked for a Tiny Tears doll and was afraid that Santa wouldn't stop at our house because we didn't have a fireplace. My brother allayed her fears and said the jolly man would use the fireplace on the clock sitting on the television set. Her little face clouded with skepticism.

"No, it's too small," she protested.

My brother wouldn't give up. "Don't worry, Santa has magic, he can go anywhere."

The next morning the Tiny Tears doll was waiting beneath the decorated tree. My sister believed the fat man had indeed slipped down the clock's tiny chimney.

Mama gave me the clock and now it's a traditional decoration in our home. It serves as a reminder of the innocence of childhood and Christmases past. Mary laughed when we remembered her Tiny Tears doll and the miniature fireplace. She believed in the magic of Santa Claus at least for that year.

Before the practice of redeeming gold, green and purple stamps died out I also hoarded books for free gifts. I remember a laundry cart used to bring in the baby diapers that dried outside in the sun. I bought gas from merchants who handed over stamps with my receipt and still have a matched set of kitchen utensils first spied in the S&H catalog. Now I carry a Furr's Frequent Shopper card and double check the tally for my savings. According to the freeway billboard over $65 million have been saved by shoppers. Smith's Food Centers has its own card but for some reason these cash savings don't have the same exciting quality of redeeming stamps.

I know there's no such thing as a free lunch but those books gave shoppers a unique way to get gifts that gained significance as the years slipped by.

September 1997

High Jumpers

◆

When former President George Bush jumped out of an airplane I spotted his wife Barbara standing by with a concerned look. Suddenly another vision flooded my mind.

Our son Rob wanted to be a free-fall jumper and trained diligently with Skydive El Paso. Every day he met with a jumpmaster to learn the details of jumping out of a Cessna 182. Rob assured us that if he froze during the jump, the 50-foot safety line would open his parachute.

That just wasn't enough; his dangerous and expensive hobby gave me heartburn. But he was paying for it and didn't ask for anything from us.

I pointed out the danger and stopped short of prohibiting his pursuit of the sport. After all, I always told our kids, "Dream big, work hard, and you can do anything you want."

So this wasn't exactly what I meant but it was his dream. I harnessed my mouth from shouting that this was definitely not what I had in mind.

As he trained for the jump I prayed a lot. If he returned home exhausted I prayed he would give it up. The next morning he headed out again while my prayers continued.

My sleeping hours were crowded with nightmares of tangled parachutes and flaming airplanes crashing to the earth. I kept silent although my stomach turned somersaults every time I thought about it.

He gave us a map to the landing area on McCombs Drive. His father was working and left me to endure the torture alone.

A cluster of people gathered to watch the event. President Bush had a lot of media coverage, my son had fellow students watching, and his mother.

My thoughts were consumed with fear and I asked God to help my son return to Earth safely.

Rob waved before disappearing into the airplane. The Cessna 182 circled in the sky before reaching the prescribed altitude of 7,000 feet. Then my child jumped out.

My heart thumped in my throat as I watched him fall through the clear blue sky. My gaze was focused on that brave young man plummeting to Earth.

"Oh, dear God, let him open the chute." I started to run, stumbled and fell. I jumped up never losing sight of my son.

Then the olive-green parachute swelled wide open. The P10 was standard military issue but the billowing green material was the most beautiful sight I had ever seen.

He descended slowly, feet touching first and then he rolled over. I ran to greet him and stopped. He'd be embarrassed if I made a scene.

Rob accepted congratulations and was shaking hands when I walked up. His face beamed when my arms flew around him. "I did it Mom." I could only nod because a huge lump had built up in my throat.

I limped away and discovered cactus needles embedded in my knee, souvenirs from the fall. Funny, I didn't feel the pain until the anxiety of Rob's jump was over. Rob made 13 subsequent jumps before he gave up the sport but that was the only one I could watch.

Perhaps Rob's adventure doesn't compare with President Bush's well-publicized jump. I forgot the camera and there are no mementos of the event.

Barbara Bush and I have something else in common, we stood by and watched a loved one fulfill a dream.

April 1997

Modesty in Shoe Repair

◆

A metallic sound rang out when the heel of my shoe struck the pavement. The rubber tip had worn out and left the metal dangerously exposed.

With every step I feared I would slip and fall on my face, or the other end. At noon I went to the Most Popular Shoe Repair and handed my shoes to the cobbler for repair.

I sat in front of a large window and tucked my stocking feet under the chair when passers-by looked in. I remembered Champion's Shoe Repair where waist-high booths offered privacy while you waited as the caps were replaced. Curtained half doors swung open to allow people in stocking feet to sit in the modest booth.

Women rushed to Champion's when the hot asphalt extracted the caps of high-heel shoes. The shop with its quaint booths was an oasis of repair if a heel broke off. I remember sitting behind the curtain hiding the runs in my stockings until my shoes were brought back to me. Then I was off to buy new hosiery. Then Champion's left the Downtown area and located at Sunrise Shopping Center for a brief time but the privacy booths with the curtained swinging doors were a thing of the past.

Downtown El Paso was left with one repair shop located on the third floor of the Popular Dry Goods Company. Mr. Romo, who was once associated with Champion's mended and resoled thousands of shoes for working men and women. Patrons sat among people rushing to hair appointments at the Beauty Salon across the aisle. The plastic molded chairs were located near the elevators and offered no place to hide your stocking feet. I walked the few paces to the counter when my shoes were ready and the cold floor sent chills up my spine. Children clinging to their mothers' skirts suspiciously eyed patrons sitting in bare feet.

For years I passed the Popular's elegant tables set with china and crystal on crisp cloths and napkins in fancy rings. Linens and towels were also displayed nearby as I headed for the shoe shop tucked in the corner on the same floor.

A yellowing bullfight poster was tacked on the wall and shoeboxes were stacked neatly on the shelves. Cowboy boots with new half-soles waited to be claimed. In the background heavy-duty sewing machines hummed as Mr. Romo and Xavier repaired leather handbags and shoes.

Every August the shop closed and that's when I most needed their services. When the shop reopened I dropped off three or four pairs of shoes in need of attention. When the rubber caps were replaced, a Popular employee delivered the shoes to my office.

I miss shopping at the Popular, having my shoes fixed and walking through the millinery department where alluring hats with filmy veils always caught my eye.

The department store closed its doors after ninety years of retailing and the cobbler relocated at 222 Texas Street. You'll find Xavier with a cheerful smile ready to put new rubber caps on worn heels while you wait. He works alone but still takes time to give my shoes a special shine. His machine almost sings when he returns to his craft and I walk off hoping that the new caps will keep me from falling on my rear end.

April 1997

One Night Affair with Sinatra

◆

Reports that Frank Sinatra is ailing released a flood of memories, for he and his music have beguiled me since I first heard him. Papa teased me about my infatuation with the crooner. "He's older than me, why do you like him?" he asked and chuckle.

Whenever Sinatra appeared on television I sang the words that persuaded lovers all over the world.

"If I see Sinatra in person I'll die happy." I said as daughter Nancy sashayed in her boots while Frank snapped his fingers to her song. Time passed and my record collection grew as Sinatra left wife Nancy and married Ava, courted Juliette, then married Mia (who chopped off her hair), and finally settled with Barbara.

In the meantime the man of my dreams captured my heart. While Bob indulged my swooning for Frank, he was never threatened. Soon Bob's Brubeck, Getz, Chicago and Bob Seeger collection crowded out my Sinatra records. My desire to see "the chairman of the board" in person never wavered.

In 1985, the Realtors' convention was held in Las Vegas. My friend Rose said, "We're going a couple of days early to catch Frank Sinatra's return from retirement, come with us," she urged knowing of my yearning.

I prepared Bob's favorite enchiladas and told him about the chance to see Sinatra, then was crushed when he said, "I have no desire to see him but you should go."

My son added, "Mom, you always said you'd die happy if you saw Sinatra, go for it."

So I went and packed a blue silk dress to wear when "old blue eyes" performed. Our El Paso troupe, Rose, her daughters Michele and Jennifer and I went to see Joan Rivers and Boyslesque the first night. The next day I broke out in hives as the event of my life approached and had to change dresses to cover up my itchy skin. At the Golden Nugget, Michele spotted Don Rickles in the lobby, but I didn't even care.

We paid $50 for tickets and the maitre'd led us to a table in the middle of the room. Rose warmed his palm with money and asked to be seated closer.

"Those tables are reserved for Mr. Sinatra's family but I'll see what I can do," he said stuffing the bills in his pocket.

The lights dimmed and the maitre'd actually came back to escort us to a ringside table. The orchestra began to play and my idol came on stage. He performed a few feet from our table and from that moment on I was oblivious to everything but the man and his song.

Yes, he was past seventy but Sinatra still had the power to make me cling to every note he sang.

"Come fly with me…" he crooned and I was ready to sprout wings. Every song was a favorite and awakened romantic memories as I practically collapsed in my seat.

He belted out "New York, New York" and brought the audience to its feet. The show was over but before departing Frank reached out to shake my hand. My fingers lingered in his, refusing to let go. Then he disappeared.

It wasn't until Jennifer asked if I still itched that I realized that Sinatra had cured me of the hives.

Old Blue eyes may be down, but his songs will linger in my heart, and lovers will sing them wherever they are. I am blessed with friends who helped make my dream come true. God Bless you Rose, and Frank too for a lifetime of wonderful music.

January 1997

The Bear, History
Maker at UTEP

◆

As Coach Don Haskins is inducted into the Basketball Hall of Fame my mind like those of others drifts back through the years remembering the joy of basketball under his direction.

When I remember the 1966 basketball season I envision Bobby Joe Hill streaking down the court like a thief in the night. The Miners kept marching on toward College Park, Md. where the final four was scheduled. Adolph Rupp's stunned demeanor when the Texas Western Miners, the Cinderella team from El Paso defeated his powerhouse team is still etched in my mind.

Back in El Paso, citizens of all ages watched proudly as the team racked up wins. During a cliffhanger of a game, someone had a heart attack from the excitement. Grocery stores and gasoline stations placed prominent signs on windows and marquees announcing the number of victories.

Then the team traveled to Washington and lost to the university in Seattle. The city was suddenly engulfed in mournful cloud but the team rebounded and emerged more energized than ever. I can almost see David Lattin's elbows flying as he fought to control the ball after a rebound. His actions were typical of the team's determination and tenacity.

As Willie Worsley, Willie Cager, Nevil Shed, David Lattin, Bobby Joe Hill and company dazzled crowds with close games, we sat glued to the television set, urging our Miners to victory.

That fateful March night when Texas Western College won the NCAA Championship we could no longer rejoice at home. We piled into the car and hit the streets, honking horns to show our joy. It was our Super Bowl. For several hours, we hung out car windows chanting "We're Number One."

The image of our team cutting the net off was an unforgettable sight. El Paso was converted into one big party and everybody took ownership of the team. Everyone wore orange, from shorts and sweaters to plastic bracelets and earrings everybody had to show their colors.

When the team returned a huge throng of people turned up at the airport where we clamored around the round ball heroes. Our old, silent, 8-millimeter home movies depict thousands of fans cheering with thousands of pointed fingers proclaiming the national championship.

Subsequent teams brought as much excitement as the Miners racked up almost 700 victories. We experienced the thrill of victory and the pain of defeat in the old Memorial Gym. Names like Nate Archibald, Tim Hardaway, Fred Reynolds, and others helped us initiate the Special Events Center where victory banners hang proudly.

We went to games, getting hoarse from cheering, then rushed home to watch a delayed replay and relive the moments that the Miners made special. Mama never understood why we would go the basketball game and then stay up late to watch it on television. But sometimes she stayed up with us too. Miner fever engulfed us all.

Now Haskins, known as the Bear, traveled to Maryland again and finally takes his place in the Hall of Fame while El Paso bursts with pride from a distance. Coach Haskins brought the entire region together with a team of basketball players. He selected the best players but took a giant leap for equality despite the sneers and comments of the small-minded.

He built a coaching dynasty enviable for its discipline and common sense and we are all better for it.

Thanks Coach, for all the wonderful games throughout the years. You earned the Hall of Fame a long time ago, now we'll see you at the Don Haskins Center, no further explanation is necessary.

October 1997

The Gramm Quacker

◆

The Great American Duck Race lured me to Deming, N. M. a couple of years ago. Our son and his wife who live in this quiet town invited us to partake in the fun.

First our son competed in the tortilla toss and won a green T-shirt. We strolled the grounds admiring handcrafts while drinking lemonade. We ate roasted corn, turkey drumsticks and swayed to the music of the band playing in the gazebo.

The duck race was open to professional aficionados, amateurs and children alike. Robert Duck, (yes, that's his real name) and a stable of aquatic birds won the big money prizes from the beginning.

Then the rules changed and professional ducks were not allowed to enter. Instead Robert Duck smiled and waved to the crowd from a red Corvette and served as grand marshal of the Great American Duck Race.

After the parade my husband Bob and I climbed up the bleachers and watched children hold squirming ducks as they waited for the race to begin.

The judges' stand was perched above eight chicken wire fenced lanes. The announcer called out names and hometowns as the kids lined up with the uneasy fowl.

The crowd laughed when a father leaned over to help a little girl retrieve a feisty duck. The man lost his balance and fell over as the duck took off.

"Ready, set, go!" the announcer said. A chain was pulled, the gates opened and the crowd roared as the feathered competitors waddled down the grassy lanes.

Soon the announcer was pleading for more competitors.

"Join in folks, we need at least five entries for each race."

Impulsively I pulled out ten dollars for the entry fee.

"I'm going to try it," I said on my way down the stands.

At the registration table a woman handed me a form and thanked me for taking up the challenge. I wrote my name address and the title for my racing partner. Gramm Quacker, I christened the bird. As a member of U. S. Senator Phil Gramm's staff I thought that would really be a hoot.

She handed me a slip that read: Race 21, Place 7. "That's your position," she responded to my quizzical look.

"Where's the duck?" I asked.

"Take the paper back there, they'll give you one." She pointed to the area behind the judges where a flock of ducks vied for space in a fenced pen.

I approached a young woman in tight jeans standing behind the fence.

"Give me a winner," I said.

She leaned down and picked up a brown duck and handed it over.

I started to walk away when something hot and wet coursed down my leg. I stopped dead in my tracks.

"It peed on me," I said turning to "tight jeans" breaking into a convulsion of giggles. Guffaws from the bleachers filled my ears as I held the duck at arm's length.

"I've got something to help you clean up," offered the teenager inside the pen. He unzipped a backpack as I rushed to his side. Pulling out a roll of toilet paper he tugged at it and handed me a wad.

"Give me the duck," he said.

I gladly turned over the web-footed creature and used the toilet paper to wipe the bird's offense off my leg. I spotted the yellow evidence of the duck's solid waste on my white high-top sneakers at the same time that my nostrils filled with his stinking smell.

"Contestants in race 21 please take your places," the announcer said.

"Wait, this lady has a duck," the teenager holding my bird hollered as I wiped off the mess.

"You have to hurry," he urged and passed the rented duck back to me.

The announcer was calling for "Gramm Quacker" when I rushed by and dropped to my knees in front of slot number seven. My hands were around the bird but my thoughts were consumed with the deposits he'd left on my shoes.

"After messing on me, you'd better win," I hissed at the dirty fowl.

The announcer shouted for the start, the gates flew open, and I let go. In a matter of seconds the racing ducks were waddling down the runway and into the pen. My part was done.

I stood up looking for Bob in the bleachers. My husband should know if my duck was the winner.

"This was tight race, folks. Duck Number One and Gramm Quaker please hold on for the results," the man at the microphone said.

I found Bob in the stands and flashed hand signals to let him know what the duck had done to me. When he laughed I knew he'd seen it all.

When the results came in, Gramm Quacker was declared the winner and I took a victorious bow. Someone handed me an envelope and I ran back up the bleachers.

My husband's greeting made me frown.

"That was good enough for 'America's Funniest Videos'"

Then he lamented, "Too bad I didn't have the Camcorder running."

"I need a bath," I said and opened the envelope.

Twenty-five dollars were tucked inside. Gramm Quacker made it a fun day and after taking a hot shower, it was worth every drop of it.

August 1995

Canciones de America

◆

It was a lazy 4th of July as I watched the stars and stripes flutter gently on the porch. Lee Greenwood sang the last chords of "God Bless the USA"

Suddenly Linda Ronstadt's music filled the air and I sang along while my son sulked. He complained that I was keeping him from listening to his new Black Crowes compact disc.

Linda's songs carried me back to a concert where the stage was alive with dancers in bright folkloric costumes. The chanteuse labeled her album *"Canciones de mi Padre,"* the songs of her father. Memories flooded back as she sang the songs Papa encouraged me to sing as he played the guitar.

When I was a child in El Paso the world revolved around my father. He sang of love, despair and sorrow with appropriate emotion. Every morning he tuned the radio to XELO's *"Gallito Madrugador,"* where a rooster's early crow awakened us before music filled the airwaves.

While Mama packed his lunch, Papa strummed the guitar to accompany his singing of a lover's conquest, unrequited love, or tales of lonely *braceros.*

Sleepily I heard verses about *"Dos Arbolitos,"* a favorite horse, or spurned love and envisioned my grandfather's journey to America. Romantic songs became my favorite as I dreamed of having my heart conquered by love.

The fascination with music spurred us to learn to read Spanish. My brother and I deciphered the words from Papa's songbook in order to harmonize with the radio. A tattered copy of *"Alma Nortena,"* published locally by Sandoval News is still treasured.

In school we sang the national anthem with fervor and joined Kate Smith's "God Bless America" on television's "Ed Sullivan Show."

Growing up we also learned "Those Caissons Go Rolling Along," and sang along with Papa, a proud Army veteran.

Our birthdays started with a serenade by Papa's quartet that included a *guitarron*, a violinist and another guitarist. Papa worked hard and returned before Mama put us to bed. We fell asleep to the sound of his music and slumbered in the security of our parents' love.

We were a happy, fun-loving family, and music obscured our poverty. We learned to tell Papa's mood by the music he played. Usually he sang romantic tunes as he stole fleeting glances at Mama, which now I understand. I watched his fingers fly over the guitar strings as he sang a silly song about a lady hiding a cat under her bed. The memory of harmonizing, "Twinkle, Twinkle, Little Star" with his rich baritone voice lingers deliciously in my mind.

Then there were times when he simply strummed the guitar with a faraway look. We recognized it as the time he preferred to be left alone.

In adolescence we gathered at the corner to sing with the street lamp as our spotlight. In the barrio guitarist friends invited me to sing because I knew the words to their favorite songs. It didn't matter that my voice was mediocre; we found solace in our musical bond.

"Sin ti, no podre vivir jamas, y pensar que nunca mas, estaras junto a mi..." Sang the mariachis on our wedding night as we looked to the future. Thirty years later, the lyrics, "without you I could never live or think that nevermore you would be at my side," have become more significant as we grow old together.

Often on the road of life we discard things carried along the way. Yesterday's songs are the baggage from my life's journey. Those happy, sad and nonsensical tunes never lost a place in my heart. My repertoire just expanded to include rock and roll, pop and jazz.

As our kids became teens, their musical choices helped us bridge the generation gap. Billy Joel, Huey Lewis, and Pink Floyd joined Sinatra, Brubeck, Los Panchos, Chicago, Linda Ronstadt, and the Beatles on our musical shelves.

Last summer I enjoyed El Paso's Mariachi Festival and paused to reflect on how blessed it is to live in a country that guarantees our right to the pursuit of happiness.

Sometimes we take freedom for granted, forgetting about nations where citizens are denied the liberty to vote, assemble, play music or complain about gangsta rap.

I'm grateful that my heritage gives me the ability to appreciate Mexican music. I thank God my grandparents who followed their dreams and guaranteed me the right to sing America's praises

July 1996

About the Author

◆

Margarita Velez is a writer from El Paso, Texas. Her columns were published in the El Paso Times. Other work appeared in the Southwest Woman, Deming Highlight and The El Paso Herald Post. She and husband Bob are parents of Robert, Laura, Michael and Vince and have five grandchildren. Velez has completed a novel.